A DASH OF DESIRE

three steamy short stories

BRIANNA BANCROFT

This is a work of fiction. Names, characters, places, and incidents either are the product of the author's imagination or are used fictitiously. Any resemblance to actual persons, living or dead, events, or locales is entirely coincidental.

Editor: Brooklyn Marie at Brazen Hearts Author Services

Cover Design: Cassie Weaver at Weaver Way Author Services

For anyone who's had to start over.

THE BUSINESSWOMAN AND THE BARTENDER

BLURB & CONTENT NOTES

April Markham might be jet-lagged beyond belief, but at least the bartender at her hotel is easy on the eyes. After years of throwing herself into work to combat the pain of a failed relationship, a bit of innocent flirtation is exactly what she needs to get her groove back.

Nick is the full package—charming, handsome, age appropriate, single. Plus, he makes a fantastic gin gimlet. One night of conversation turns into two, and his company quickly becomes as irresistible as the cocktails he crafts. Although April never intended to mix business with pleasure while traveling for work, things are destined to move from the bar to the bedroom.

But as the red-hot flame of attraction burns bright, reality threatens to douse their heat. She's a businesswoman from New York; he's a bartender in Seattle. And as her flight home looms, April must decide whether to risk her heart on a cross-country affair or announce "last call" on what could be the romance of a lifetime.

Content Notes: explicit sex, parental death (breast cancer, off page), parental illness (stroke, off page)

ONE

Jet lag was a killer.

It was only seven in the evening, but April Markham could barely keep her eyes open. She'd been awake hours before the sun for an early six-thirty flight out to Seattle, only to sit on the grounded plane at JFK for two hours, delayed because of a light bulb that blew before takeoff.

By the time she finally arrived in the Emerald City, she was thankful to hear that her hotel room was ready early. She napped for a few hours, hoping that a quick bit of shut-eye would reset her inner clock. Yet she struggled to stay sharp as she headed down to one of the hotel's restaurants. She'd traveled often enough for business to know she had to push through the fatigue, make it through dinner, and nurse a few cocktails before finally passing out for the night.

A chorus of happy chatter filled the lobby as she approached the steakhouse in the hotel, praying a spot would be available at the bar. While she had no problem dining alone—was truthfully used to it by this point in her life—she preferred eating at the bar instead of taking up an entire table in a restaurant. Fortunately, the lounge area was quieter, with only one person at the bar and a few clusters of people at high-top tables. The space was separate from the main dining room, complete with low lighting and sophisticated touches. Plush stools lined the bar, and a large bookcase stretched across the back wall, filled with trinkets and antique tomes. It was as if she'd stumbled into the library in a gothic manor, and she loved every inch of it.

She settled on the stool at the far side of the counter and glanced over at the bartender, who was chatting with the other patron at the bar. When he looked her way, her stomach leaped unexpectedly.

Oh, he was *cute*—albeit a little young at first glance. He was of decent height, around six foot, with a shade of light-brown hair that was nondescript and average but somehow suited him perfectly. He was the epitome of all-American good looks, complete with a body undeniably in shape but not obnoxiously ripped.

As he moved toward her, her focus subtly dipped to his left hand. *No ring.* That didn't mean much when discerning his relationship status, but checking for a ring had become a natural habit the older she got.

"Evening," he greeted with a friendly smile, his dimples emerging like a sneak attack. "Dinner? Drinks?"

She returned the smile and said, "Both."

He nodded and passed her a gilded booklet. "This is our dinner menu. Specialty cocktails are on the back page. But I can make almost anything you'd like."

"I'll take a gin gimlet, please."

"Any gin preference?" He filled a glass with ice water and placed it in front of her.

"I'm not picky. Whatever you suggest."

"You got it."

As he prepared her drink, she perused the menu. Since

she was traveling on behalf of her job, she expensed her meals, and the best part was that her company didn't require itemized receipts. Still, she knew better than to run up an insanely expensive dinner bill, and she usually opted for a smaller plate or salad so she could indulge in more alcoholic beverages. She had business travel down to a science by now.

The bartender tossed a cocktail napkin onto the sleek onyx bar and placed the gimlet down with a flourish. "My favorite is the steak sandwich," he said. "But if you're looking for a salad, the wedge is probably our most popular."

The wedge salad was what she'd had her eye on, and his recommendation solidified her choice. She snapped the menu shut and ordered that before taking a sip of her cocktail. "Oh, that's good," she praised with a sigh.

Butterflies flapped in her stomach as his heady laugh echoed between them. "Glad you approve. I'll put your food order in. It shouldn't take too long to come out."

"Great, thank you."

Their fingers brushed when she handed the menu back to him. The light touch sent a delightful shiver through her body, and her eyes shot up to find his gaze. Such an innocent caress, but it didn't go unnoticed by him. The masculine column of his throat bobbed as he swallowed thickly. They both averted eye contact, rife with awkwardness, as he placed the menu to the side.

In her periphery, April saw a couple take a seat at the bar. The bartender noticed as well, and soon they'd moved past the brief and unintentional touch. Before he went to greet the new customers, he gave her one last dazzling smile and said, "My name's Nick, by the way. Let me know if you need anything."

She nodded demurely as he sauntered to the other end

of the bar to welcome the new arrivals. Watching discreetly, April observed his easygoing charm—a facet all excellent bartenders possessed. Clad in respectable black dress pants and a white button-down shirt—ostensibly his work uniform—there was still an enticing roughness to him. A hint that he'd be just as comfortable wearing flannel while riding a dirt bike or hiking trails in the Pacific Northwest. She imagined how satisfying it would be to rub her face against his firm chest, feeling the soft fabric against her cheek as they lounged by a roaring fire. A fire filled with wood he'd chopped himself, like those lumberjack social media personalities who slammed an axe down while shirtless. Not that she followed any of those guys religiously or anything.

Christ, she was pretty hard up if she was already imagining romantic scenarios with a man she'd uttered only a few words to. Sure, he wasn't wearing a ring, but he must have a partner of some sort. It was impossible for someone that classically handsome to be single. Not to mention she guessed he was in his late twenties. Some might say age is nothing but a number, but April couldn't imagine being romantically involved with anyone that much younger than her own age of thirty-five—even if it was only for one night.

A burst of laughter sounded from a group at a table behind her, a blunt indication that she was ill-advised to fall victim to lofty fantasies while in public. Shaking off the silliness, she pulled out her work phone and skimmed emails that came in earlier that day despite her out-of-office automatic reply. There was nothing super pressing in her inbox, so she opted to wait to answer the correspondence until she returned.

Smooth and sexy jazz echoed throughout the space, contrasting hilariously with the basketball game playing on the wall-mounted television at the far end of the bar. April relaxed into her chair, wiggling against the cushiony velvet of the stool, as she enjoyed the tangy and sweet taste of her gimlet. Never one to actively follow sports, she pretended to care about the basketball game as she waited for her dinner; otherwise, she'd gawk at the bartender all night long.

Soon enough, Nick returned with the salad and a set of utensils. "Fresh ground pepper?"

"Please," she said, trying to focus on anything other than his large hands as they worked the mahogany pepper mill. After a few turns, she signaled she was good, and he pulled the mill away.

"Enjoy."

"Thank you."

He returned to his work, and she tucked into her salad, which was simple but still delicious. Once finished, she placed her utensils atop the plate and pushed it forward to return her full attention to her cocktail, which was nearing the bottom of the coupe glass.

Nick noticed and headed over, removing the plate and placing it behind the bar. "Another gimlet?" he asked.

"Yes, please."

"How was your salad?"

"It was exactly what I needed," she said. "It's funny, though. I hate bleu cheese. But it's so satisfying on a wedge salad."

He poured the gin into the cocktail shaker, looking absurdly sexy while doing so. "Same here. I feel like bleu cheese only works in a wedge salad or with chicken wings. Other than that, you can keep it."

"Agreed." After a pause, she rubbed her eyes. "What a weird thing to bring up. Can you tell I'm jet-lagged?"

Laughing, he shook her cocktail vigorously, the slamming of the ice adding to the cacophony of the lounge. His biceps bulged against the white shirtsleeves, which made her mouth ridiculously parched.

"I'm a bartender. There's no such thing as a weird conversation when you're in this line of work."

"Fair enough."

"Where you visiting from?" he asked.

"New York."

"No wonder you're jet-lagged. Business or pleasure?"

Her libido jumped at that question—*both, please!*

"Technically business," she admitted. "I have a conference starting tomorrow. But I added an extra day to the trip so I can do some touristy things."

He strained the drink into a new glass and set it atop the cocktail napkin. "Let me guess. Space Needle?"

She smiled sheepishly. "I may have already purchased a ticket."

He grinned back and maintained her gaze. His eyes were the dark gray-blue color of a storm cloud. April had often heard the sentiment that some people looked at others so raptly that you'd believe there was no one else in the room. She'd never experienced the phenomenon before. Not until this moment.

But as quickly as it began, the intoxicating episode ended. Nick detected another patron raising their chin toward him to signal that they needed either their bill or another round. "Enjoy your gimlet," he said before walking over to the other side of the bar.

And enjoy she did, even though the alcohol added to her fatigue. The easy conversation with Nick, coupled with his undeniable good looks, had given her a shot of adrenaline, but any energy she'd possessed waned as she sipped away at her second drink. She glanced at her watch. It was nine thirty. If she could push through until ten, she'd have a good chance of getting a decent night's sleep.

Despite the encroaching exhaustion, electricity ripped through her moments later when she noticed Nick staring from the other end of the bar. Her attention darted to his rugged hands as he used a cloth to thoroughly polish a wine glass, his movements methodical and self-possessed. An onslaught of dirty fantasies inundated her brain, and she suddenly found herself jealous of a mere wine glass.

A wine glass, of all things.

The right corner of his lips kicked into an alluring smirk, one deep dimple on display, as he strode back and refilled her water glass. "You said you're here for a conference. What do you do?" he asked.

Lust-addled thoughts rendered her tongue-tied for a few seconds. "Uh, I work in business development for a pharmaceutical company."

"You like it?"

She shrugged. "It pays the bills."

He dipped his head in understanding. "I know how that is."

There were a few sips left in her gimlet, and she wasn't sure she could continue this conversation without making a fool of herself in front of him. "I'm going to crash after I finish this. Can I settle up?"

"Of course." He walked over to the POS system and printed out her bill, placing it down in front of her. "Take your time."

April quickly reviewed the charges and slipped her corporate credit card into the pocket at the top of the folio. Nick was wiping down the bar, but when he saw she was ready, he returned and ran her card.

"I hope you enjoy Seattle," he said, handing her back her credit card and printed receipt.

"Thanks. I'm sure I will."

He returned to tidying up, and she tipped him in cash before going on her way.

Just another friendly conversation with a bartender. Thanks to the regular travel her job required, she'd had dozens of similar interactions throughout the years. But none had made her stomach flutter so fiercely.

And no other bartender had invaded her dreams. Because that night, she dreamed that she was standing in the hotel's elevator. And when the doors to the lift opened, Nick walked in. He said not a word to her. They simply stared at each other until he stepped forward and shot his hand down to cup her between her legs, pressing the fingers that had deftly crafted her cocktails straight against the most sensitive part of her.

She awoke with a start. In the darkness, her eyes found the clock on the nightstand, and a dejected sigh left her lungs. It was three in the morning, which meant it was six on the East Coast—the typical time she awakened.

So much for beating jet lag.

TWO

The first day of the conference was a success. April had two client meetings, one of which was over lunch. They dined at a dumpling house not far from the convention center, and then the conference officially kicked off that afternoon with several seminars. Between the forums, she had a few quick chats with the usual suspects. Conferences were similar to family reunions in a way. You saw the same people, caught up on typical personal and professional topics, and did it all again the following year.

That evening, she dodged a dinner invitation from two of her coworkers. Being social all day was exhausting, and all she wanted was a quiet meal. Especially since there was one more day of the conference to endure.

And was she secretly hoping a certain handsome bartender would serve her again?

Perhaps.

She'd worn casual clothing the night before—jeans and a shapeless sweater—and her thick chestnut hair had been pulled up in a ponytail. But today she was in her best business casual: navy dress pants that hugged her natural curves, a cream blouse with bishop sleeves, and modest sling-back heels that added a few inches to her average height. Since she'd been up early that morning, she'd air-dried her naturally wavy hair and had painstakingly applied her makeup, taking time to highlight her upturned hazel eyes with eyeshadow and mascara. She looked good and felt even better, and she could only hope that Nick was working and would agree.

The lounge area was considerably busier, and there was an additional cocktail waitress working the space. April's heels clacked against the tile floor as she approached the bar, the sound a siren call as Nick immediately looked her way. His eyes lit with recognition as she hoisted herself into the same stool she'd occupied the prior evening.

"Hey." The one-word greeting teemed with intimacy, his voice low and husky. "I served you last night, right? Gin gimlet?"

"That's right. Good memory."

Nick handed her a menu and lifted one shoulder in an easy shrug. "You were memorable."

Her face burned hotter than the sun's surface in response to that compliment. With a light laugh, she glanced down at the menu to get her bearings straight. "I'm a creature of habit. I'll have another gimlet."

"Coming right up."

As he prepared her drink, she tried to settle her rioting belly. But it was difficult to do when the simple sight of his hands enthralled her and brought last night's dream barreling back to the forefront of her mind. How he'd stepped forward and cupped the space between her legs so surely, without even asking for permission, as if that was where he belonged. It was a testament to how long she'd been alone that a few seconds of fantasy could set her blood on fire and consume her thoughts hours later.

He set the coupe glass down and asked, "Doing dinner again?"

Only if dessert is you. She mentally swatted away that unhinged thought and choked out a response. "Uh, yes. Yesterday you said you like the steak sandwich?"

"I eat it an unhealthy amount," he admitted, a cheeky grin on his face.

"I'll do that, then."

With a quick nod, he took her menu and put her order in. Her seat was closest to his main workstation, so it provided a clear view of him even though he couldn't chat. The busy atmosphere meant that his top priority was churning drinks out constantly for the bargoers and the waitresses working the tables. There was something magnetic about his movements, a fluidity that was as graceful as a dancer and as assertive as a man who knew how to handle a willing woman.

It was fascinating to watch him craft cocktail after cocktail. Martini, old fashioned, margarita, mojito, cosmopolitan —drink after drink after drink. It was clear he was a natural at his chosen vocation. He was able to expertly create drinks, take food orders, direct the barback, and do it all while shooting the shit with customers.

To save face—and not continue to stare like a stalker—she nursed her gimlet and scrolled through social media on her phone. And maybe a lumberjack video or two. Soon her steak sandwich arrived, brought over by the barback instead of Nick. But he was right behind the food runner with a set of utensils for her.

"Can I get you anything else?" he asked.

April shook her head. "I'm good. Thanks, Nick."

His cheerful face shifted to a different expression—as if using his name demonstrated that she'd also found him memorable, and that was particularly satisfying to him.

"What was your name again?"

"Oh, it's April. I don't think I properly introduced myself yesterday."

He waved his hand, telling her not to worry. "You were jet-lagged."

Another thing he'd remembered about her. It made her impossibly warm all over.

"Enjoy your meal," he said.

The steak sandwich was perfectly cooked and exactly what she needed after a day of being on the go. While at the other end of the bar, Nick looked over and caught her eye. His eyebrows raised in question, and she gave him a thumbs up, signaling that the sandwich was as good as he'd promised. He winked in response, and she nearly whimpered at the flirtatious gesture.

She needed to get a hold of herself. But the truth was, it felt like an eternity since she'd indulged in a bit of flirting. When her one meaningful relationship had ended five years ago, she'd thrown herself into work. After being with her college sweetheart for so long, she'd lost her identity and had wanted to remove men from the equation entirely until she figured out who she really was. Her career flourished as the years passed, but she realized her dedication to the journey of self-discovery meant she'd shut out even the possibility of a new relationship. Now the idea felt downright foreign, and, in some ways, she was no different from an inexperienced teenager.

Her heart ricocheted against her sternum each time he returned to his workstation to prepare a drink order. So painfully close, despite the gleaming bar between them.

After he crafted two martinis—one with a twist and one dirty—his long fingers pulled the next order slip from the tiny printer, and he set to work on an old fashioned, dashing bitters into a lowball glass.

The reemergence of his throaty voice jolted her concentration back to his face. "So, April...you probably get this a lot, but were you born in April?"

She did get it a lot; so much so that she typically rolled her eyes at the question, but coming from Nick, it made her downright giddy. "My mother's due date was April seventh. She'd already had her heart set on my name when my stubborn self decided to come early. My birthday's March thirty-first."

He chuckled and handed the old fashioned over to the second waitress. "Keeping people on their toes from the beginning, huh?"

"Something like that."

Her sandwich hadn't stood a chance, the plate practically licked clean, so he removed it and asked if she wanted another drink. She certainly wasn't about to call it an early night—not when he was indulging her with a bit of attention—so she nodded, and he got to work on her gimlet.

"You're busy tonight," she observed.

"Yeah. Hopefully, it starts to clear out soon. I assume a lot of these people are from your conference?"

A few faces were recognizable, although none she was familiar enough with that she felt required to join. "Probably. But the conference ends tomorrow evening, and people usually depart right after. Things might be quieter for you. Unless you're not working then?"

Yes, she was fishing. Sue her.

"Oh, I'm here all week," he confirmed. "No rest for the wicked."

There was a heated twinkle in his eye as he set her drink down before moving to check on the rest of his customers.

April, for the love of God, you need to get a grip. The man was a bartender. It was his job to make her feel welcome and special. And the more flirtatious he was, the more likely he was to get a good tip. It wasn't rocket science.

Still, where was the harm? Maybe this was exactly what she needed to thaw her and get her back in the habit of meeting men. While she wasn't keen to return to the bar scene of her college days, and the idea of going on a dating app made her want to pull her hair out, she had to take baby steps. A bit of frivolity with a cute bartender was just the thing to accomplish that. Even if he was surely in a relationship and too damn young for her.

People began to clear out around nine thirty. Her second gimlet was almost finished, but she wasn't ready to go yet—especially if fewer customers meant he'd have more time to chat with her. She sipped at the ice water, hoping it wasn't insanely obvious that she was purposefully lingering.

A pair of women were soon the only ones left at the bar besides herself. As Nick conversed with them, April kept her attention on the television—basketball again—but eavesdropped on the conversation.

"How handsome you are," one of the women mused. "Are you single?"

"Indeed I am. You looking to wine and dine me?" Nick joked.

The ladies tittered at his teasing. "No, but my niece would."

Stunned by the knowledge that he was single, April immediately wanted to sabotage any chance for this faceless niece to sink her claws into Nick, but she composed herself and let common sense return. It was ludicrous to get territorial over someone she'd never see again.

"She's a sweet girl," the woman continued. "She's twenty-four, a dental assistant, and loves dogs."

"Ah, a little too young for me, I'm afraid," Nick replied regretfully.

Another jolt of surprise struck April. Twenty-four was too young for him?

The women expressed their disappointment despite accepting his answer. Nick topped off their glasses, finishing the bottle of red wine they were sharing. As he sorted through receipts, April kept her focus on the television, trying to act natural and not betray how her heart was galloping like a prized racehorse.

He was single. Fair game. The perfect specimen for a vacation fling. She didn't care if his flirting was simply pleasant bartender banter, and she didn't care if she was another woman in the long line of women he flirted with each night. She was buzzed enough after two gimlets to concoct a foolhardy scheme.

Seduce him. Easy enough, right?

When he turned back toward her, she stilled her features. He placed his forearms down on the bar and leaned in as if they were old confidants. "Can I tempt you with another?"

She pretended to consider it, tapping one finger against her chin. His smirk widened into a genuine smile at her coyness.

"Tempt away," she drawled.

He nodded once with approval and grabbed a cocktail shaker. "This one's on me."

"Oh, you don't have to do that—"

"I insist. As thanks for keeping me company tonight."

"What time do you usually close?" she asked.

"It depends on the night and how busy we are. Anywhere between ten and eleven is pretty standard. Later on the weekends, obviously."

"Well, please tell me if I overstay my welcome."

Nick planted her third gimlet of the night down on the bar and held her stare. "That could never happen," he answered softly.

Her chest tightened, infatuation growing and taking root. And that was to say nothing of her panties, which were undeniably damp. She shifted a bit and clenched her thighs together.

A part of her was grateful that he was technically still working, as she could collect herself between their bouts of heated flirtation. As he settled the bill for the other two women at the bar, the absence of boisterous chatter caused April to turn her head.

The lounge was nearly empty. Only one couple at a high-top table and a group of four people tucked away in the corner remained. The cocktail waitresses settled up the remaining parties' bills and departed, saying their goodbyes to Nick. It was so quiet that April could almost pretend they were alone in her hotel room with the door bolted and a do-not-disturb sign hanging from the knob.

"Those ladies were funny." He nodded in the direction of where the older women had sat. "Did you catch any of their conversation?"

Oh Lord, it must have been obvious she'd eavesdropped. She came clean and admitted, "A bit. Were they trying to set you up with someone?"

His cheeks tinted pink as he loaded the dishwasher rack with used glasses. "Yeah, they were."

"You must get that a lot."

He peered at her measuredly and eventually said, "Sometimes. But not that often, trust me."

April traced a finger up and down the stem of her glass. "You gonna go for it? Let the sweet old biddy play matchmaker?"

Shaking his head, he placed the rack in the washer and turned it on. "Too young. Dating anyone younger than thirty creeps me out."

"Wait, how old *are* you?" she blurted, gin and curiosity taking over.

"Thirty-seven."

That answer about knocked her over. "You look...uh, much younger than that," she finished awkwardly.

He smiled, and she finally noticed the faint wrinkles around his eyes instead of hyper-focusing on the irresistible dimples. She'd made up her mind so quickly about him—and how unsuitable he was for her—that she hadn't noticed telltale signs that he wasn't some young pretty boy.

"It's because I'm clean-shaven. I look more my age when I grow a beard out. But they like to keep a certain aesthetic around here," he told her, gesturing to the establishment.

She nodded absently, still a little thrown. Not only was he cute and single, but he was also age appropriate? It seemed too good to be true.

"The one in the red sweater reminded me of my mom," he murmured, and it took April a moment to realize he was referring to one of the potential matchmakers who'd recently left. "Same mannerisms and everything."

There was something particularly sweet about hearing a grown man talk of his mother with such respect and affection in his voice. "Does she live locally?" she asked.

"She did. She passed last summer."

Her stomach plummeted to the center of the earth. "Oh, Nick. I'm so sorry."

His gaze found hers, sorrow still lingering in his eyes. "Thanks. She..." He paused, and April wanted to launch over the bar and hug him. "Breast cancer. Same old story. But not, at the same time."

"Of course." She understood that sentiment all too well. "It's sobering, isn't it? You think your parents are invincible, even as you get older. And then suddenly—"

"They're not," he finished for her with a thoughtful tilt of his head.

"My dad had a minor stroke two months ago," she admitted quietly. "He's fine, thank God. But it was the first time it hit me that my parents won't be around forever."

"Yeah. It shouldn't have come as a shock—she'd been sick for months—but the day she died, I was completely stunned. Didn't seem real." He cleared his throat and said, "Sorry. You don't want to hear all this depressing stuff."

How wrong he was. She wanted to hear it—wanted to learn everything she could about him. Without thinking, she reached forward and grabbed his hand. It was different from the harmless skim of their fingers the night prior. It was deliberate and personal, and it might have been too familiar, considering they'd only just met, but April was compelled to offer him a bit of comfort.

"Nothing to be sorry for," she assured him, giving his hand a supportive squeeze before releasing it. "Are you close with your dad, at least?"

He smiled fondly. "I am. We're buds. Losing her was hard for him, but the grief helped bring us closer in this weird way."

"Silver lining."

They shared a meaningful stare until he ducked his head and asked, "So, you a native New Yorker?"

She couldn't blame him for changing the subject. "I'm originally from Pennsylvania. But I moved to the city for college when I was eighteen. Been there ever since."

"What do you think of Seattle? You're lucky you're getting good weather this week."

"Not that I've gotten to enjoy it much, being stuck in the convention center all day. Hopefully, it will still be nice on my day off. But so far, I like what I see."

She hadn't intended for that final sentence to be loaded with innuendo, but best-laid plans and whatnot. He caught her gaze and murmured, "I'm glad."

April cleared her throat to try and recalibrate. "Anyway. What do you suggest I check out while I'm here?"

"Pike Place Market, naturally. And if you have time, the boat rides around the bay are fun and not too expensive. Oh, and there's this fantastic steakhouse I can recommend."

There was a teasing lilt to his voice, and she played along. "You don't say."

"Great food. Bartender's a bit of a dork, though."

She laughed heartily, but before she could retort with a snappy comeback, their conversation was interrupted by the barback, who needed assistance in the storage room. Nick excused himself and left her alone. She peered over her shoulder and saw that the last groups of people had departed, making her officially the last one standing.

Not only that, but she was tipsy. Nowhere near blackout drunk, but still buzzed enough that the depressive effects of alcohol flourished, and her insecurity flared in the silence.

God, how pathetic was she? Hanging around like a dog in heat, desperate for a bit of attention. This wasn't a date, and she would do well to remember that. She rubbed her eyes with the palms of her hands, unconcerned that she was likely smudging whatever was left of her mascara.

April steeled herself and asked for the check when he finally returned to the bar, essentially destroying her seduction scenario before it had even begun.

"Of course," he answered, his eyebrows raising somewhat in response to her abrupt change of pace. He presented her with the bill and then ran her credit card.

Silence stretched between them, filling her with unease until she rambled out an excuse. "I just realized how late it is. I have to be up early again tomorrow."

Nick gave her a tender smile. "Totally get it. Working with a hangover is never fun."

"No, it's not." She paused and placed her credit card back in her purse. "Thanks again."

"Anytime." He wiped down the bar and viewed her through hooded eyes. "Hopefully, I'll see you again."

"Oh, probably. I'm staying here, you know. In this hotel. So it's convenient, obviously. Easier to come down here, get a bite, and then go back up to my room instead of heading out into the city and making the trip back. That's what I mean by convenient. If that wasn't, uh, clear."

He listened to her meandering with an amused expression. Then he let out a tsk-tsk and said, "And yet not one word about the incredible service."

Even after her bout of word vomit, he was still decent and charming and effortlessly handsome. His gentle teasing made her relax. She sighed wistfully and said, "That too. Of course. This was great. You're great, Nick."

His head dipped a bit to avoid her sincere gaze, as if maintaining eye contact was too much for him. Until he returned his gray-blue eyes to her hazel ones and silently held her stare.

It was a *moment*. There was no other way she knew how to describe it. Regardless of how the alcohol swirled within her and wreaked havoc on her emotions, the energy between them was so palpable, she couldn't deny that this small cluster of seconds *meant* something.

At least it did to her. He'd probably forget it by tomorrow.

"You're pretty great yourself. Thanks again for keeping me company," he murmured.

April knew she had to depart before humiliating herself further. She threw her purse over her shoulder and stepped down off the stool. "Have a good night."

"You too, April," he said as she turned and left the lounge. "Sleep well."

Her legs were jelly as she proceeded to the elevator bay, her entire body vibrating with intensity. As she rode the lift up to the twenty-eighth floor, she pulled out her phone and sent a drunken text to her best friend, Lucy.

> Apologies for the late-night text, but I have a huge crush on the bartender here. Like, stars in my eyes, infatuated beyond belief. Tell me to stop being dumb!

Knowing she wouldn't get a response anytime soon, seeing as it was after one in the morning on the East Coast, April tossed her phone into her purse and tottered into her hotel room. She let slumber take her, hoping she and Dream-Nick might progress to the next level. Since that was all she'd ever have of him.

THREE

Faint vibration woke her the next morning. Groaning, April flailed around in the dark until she found her cell on the nearby nightstand, still plugged into the charger. The alarm clock read four thirty, the illuminated numbers an unrelenting assault on her sleepy eyes. Her phone's bright background was even worse, pulling another miserable groan from her. But a text message from Lucy coaxed her into unlocking the screen.

You better fuck that bartender.

April guffawed and then chucked the phone to the other side of her king-sized hotel bed, allowing herself to indulge in a few more hours of sleep. Her first seminar wasn't until nine, so she'd set her alarm for seven. She hadn't dreamed of Nick that night, but she fell back asleep to the image of his smiling face in her mind, which was better than nothing.

When her alarm sounded a few hours later, she hauled herself out of bed and chugged a bottle of water. She wasn't horrifically hungover, but she was definitely feeling the effects of last night's three gimlets.

After a rejuvenating shower, she pulled her hair up into a bun and applied her makeup. Historically, the last day of a conference was always more laid back, with people dressing down. She consulted the clothes she'd packed and settled on a pair of tapered black pants, a plain white tee, and an oversized salmon-colored blazer. She slipped her feet into her favorite black loafers, grabbed her purse and name badge, and headed out to the last day of the conference.

The morning consisted of dull seminars and one more client meeting. Then April met her two coworkers for lunch at a café a few blocks away from the convention center. While slurping her soup, she checked her personal phone and saw a follow-up text from Lucy.

You haven't answered me. I hope it's because you're doing the nasty.

April snorted with laughter and typed out:

It's one in the afternoon!

Lucy's reply arrived in record time:

Your point?

I asked you to tell me to stop being dumb. Not to encourage me.

Ah, but what are friends for?

Shaking her head with mirth, she placed her phone back in her purse and geared up for the final stretch of sessions. Both of her coworkers were booked on red-eye flights and bound for home that night, poised to leave soon after the last seminar concluded at six in the evening. She said a quick goodbye to them, as well as a few others, before heading back to her hotel.

Her stomach twisted with hunger, and she knew she should go somewhere else for dinner. Seattle had hundreds of incredible restaurants, and she was limiting herself from experiencing the city fully—all because of a man who wouldn't remember her once she left in a few days' time. So, after returning to her hotel room, she hardened her heart and consulted the list of nearby hot spots the hotel had supplied upon check-in. There was a highly rated Italian restaurant around the corner. Decision made, she changed her shoes, pulling on a pair of white sneakers, and exited the hotel.

The restaurant was light and airy and sported an expansive curved bar. The bartender—a woman about her age—greeted her warmly. April ordered a glass of white wine since she was certain to order pasta, and nothing paired better, in her opinion. And also because, by this point, having a gin gimlet prepared by anyone other than Nick didn't feel right.

The lobster ravioli was decadent and insanely delicious. Halfway through the meal, her cell phone buzzed with another message from Lucy.

WELL?

Shouldn't you be asleep?

Don't make me get on a plane and come over there.

I'm...conflicted.

About what? April, you've been working yourself to the bone for years now. You deserve to have a little fun!

I know, I know...I guess I'm out of practice and feeling a bit insecure.

Oh, to hell with that. You're funny and pretty and kind, and he should be honored you wanna bang his brains out.

April laughed and stabbed a ravioli with her fork. Since her decision to have dinner elsewhere, she'd been wavering on whether to stop at the bar for a nightcap or avoid it altogether. God, she was the epitome of a flip-flopper. One night she was determined to seduce Nick, and the next, she was avoiding him completely. Further proof she was out of her element.

She replied back to Lucy with a vague **I guess I'll have to see what happens** and then finished up her meal. It was a few minutes to ten o'clock as she traveled back to the hotel, and her gut churned with the possibility that they'd done last call. She remembered Nick mentioning how they decided closing time based on how busy the night was, and the idea that they'd already packed it up for the night made her feel ill.

Well, that reaction certainly spoke volumes. It was foolish to think she'd be able to head right back to her room without even looking at him. Walking as fast as her legs would allow without breaking into a full-out run, she headed to the lounge. As she approached the entrance, she caught Nick's eye from behind the bar. She watched as his chest rose and then fell, inhaling and exhaling deeply. Meanwhile, she could barely pull air into her lungs.

But somehow, she was able to move her legs, and she

approached her usual stool. The bar and lounge were nearly empty. There were two lone men sitting at the bar—one at the far end and one smack in the middle—and two parties at high-top tables. Everyone was either engrossed in their phones or in their conversations, creating the illusion of privacy as Nick drew closer.

"Hey," he said.

"Hi. You, uh, haven't done last call yet, have you?"

He shook his head and gestured for her to take a seat. "Gimlet?"

"Please."

April heaved herself up onto the stool as he prepared her cocktail. A significant silence descended around them, although the soft jazz soundtrack offered some reprieve. She had hoped that after a glass of wine, she'd be more chatty, more uninhibited, but the air was fraught.

He slid her gimlet over and murmured, "For a minute there, I was worried you weren't going to show."

She winced and avoided his gaze. "I had dinner plans."

"Ah. Clients, coworkers?"

"Yes. Exactly."

He deserved to hear the truth—that she'd avoided coming here because she was already halfway obsessed with him—but she pushed the confession down with a sip of the cocktail, which was perfectly chilled and tart.

"I'm afraid you've ruined gin gimlets for me," she blurted out.

His mouth curled and he leaned down, setting his forearms on the bar. "How so?"

"It'll feel weird drinking one that's not made by you."

The smile on his face transformed into an expression of astonishment, the dimples disappearing as his jaw sagged.

But he recovered quickly and asked, "How did the last day of the conference go?"

"Same as it ever was. How has your night been? Was it busy earlier?"

"Not too bad. Steady, for the most part, but it started to clear out about thirty minutes ago."

"I'm glad I made it in time."

He held her stare, and she had to believe, in that quiet moment, that everything leading up to this wasn't basic bartender flirtation. She hadn't misread the situation. There was something more here—something worth pursuing.

But it was also something that couldn't last. He lived in Seattle. She had made a home in New York. A one-night stand would be the extent of it. And yet, April remembered Lucy's encouraging text messages. She had to allow herself to let loose. If she wanted to have a torrid vacation fling, it should be with someone she enjoyed talking to and found genuinely attractive.

Before she could formulate how to proposition him, Nick moved to the next topic of conversation. "Excited for your tourist day tomorrow?" he asked.

"I am. I purchased a ticket for the boat tour you mentioned. Thanks for the suggestion."

He nodded in response to her gratitude. "And you fly out on Saturday?"

It was a stark reminder. If she was going to do this—follow through and seduce him—she had only tonight or tomorrow to do it.

"I do," she uttered quietly.

"Your partner must be missing you."

A record scratch sounded in her brain. "Partner?"

"Romantic partner," he supplied. "Boyfriend, girlfriend? Or as the kids like to say, your boo?"

If she wasn't stunned by the question, she would have laughed at how adorable he sounded using the term *boo*. Instead, she blinked rapidly and took a few seconds to respond. Had he spent the past two days thinking *she* was involved with someone?

Served her right.

"Oh, there's no partner," she jabbered. "No pets either. And no houseplants. I've killed every plant anyone's ever gotten for me. Nope. It's only me. No one else."

"Ah." He scratched the back of his neck. "I just assumed."

"I assumed with you too." One shoulder raised in a guilty shrug. "That first night I was here? I thought you were a young'un *and* assumed you were taken."

"And you were wrong on both counts," he teased.

"I guess I'm not a good judge of character."

"Nah, I don't believe that at all." A flash of movement from the other end of the bar caught his eye, and he said, "Excuse me for a second."

Their conversation had been so intimate that she'd completely forgotten he was still working. He told the other patrons at the bar that it was last call and supplied them with one final beer. Then he gave the cocktail waitress the signal, and she alerted the parties in the lounge that it was time to get their last round of drinks in.

One group closed out, and the other asked for one more round, which Nick prepared. As he stood at the workstation and strained a sidecar into a coupe glass, he peered over at April and said, "You don't have to rush out of here, by the way."

The statement was likely in response to how she'd taken two hefty gulps of her gimlet after hearing it was last call. It was a knee-jerk reaction, born from years of chugging drinks at her local watering hole to get one more in before closing. But at this point, she definitely couldn't stomach another cocktail.

As if he'd read her mind, he poured a glass of ice water and placed it beside the gimlet. "Feel free to hang out if you want," he added. His tone was casual, but nothing about the offer felt as such.

She nodded silently as the cocktail waitress returned to pick up the final round of drinks. Nick moved to the long counter along the back of the bar space, where every spirit under the sun lived. He brought the bottles back to their proper home, then turned his attention to the open bottles of wine and used a vacuum pump to remove air from the bottles to keep the wine as fresh as possible.

The waitress popped behind the bar and helped with a few more tasks before asking, "You mind if I bounce?"

He shook his head. "Go ahead. Jimmy's in the back. He and I can handle it."

"Awesome," the waitress said. She left in record time, leaving April alone with Nick.

While he was at the POS system, closing things up for the night, she called out, "Oh, how much do I owe you for this?"

"Nothing."

"Nick, come on."

He turned and raised an eyebrow at her. She was reminded of her dream—how he'd stared at her and had said so much with only a look.

"I'll give you a good tip," she promised in a mumble.

Once again, she hadn't meant to infuse innuendo into her message, but it seemed to happen without even trying. And when naked hunger flashed over his face, she flushed furiously.

He quickly turned away and focused on the night's receipts. But the change in his body language was unmistakable. Tension permeated from his form, the muscles in his back rigid against the cotton of his button-down shirt. One fist was clenched until he unfurled his hand and rubbed the nape of his neck, which appeared to be one of his nervous habits.

A few sexually charged minutes passed in silence. There was an unspoken understanding in the air that they both had to compose themselves, that they had to allow the electricity to lessen, lest it incinerate them both. But eventually, he returned to leaning against the bar.

"What do you have against houseplants, huh?" he joked.

She barked a laugh and then slapped a hand over her mouth in mortification. But he apparently found her over-the-top reaction endearing because he laughed softly and gave her a look that could only be described as *heart eyes*.

"Even the plants know I'm too independent for my own good," she mumbled.

His eyes narrowed as he considered that answer. "That's an interesting way to put it. Too independent for your own good?"

The wine from dinner, coupled with gin, released the floodgates. "I spent a lot of time working on myself. To make sure I was strong on my own. Capable. But that sort of consumed me to the point where now it's hard to even imagine letting someone into my life. Even plants," she finished half-heartedly.

"Let me guess. You were in a long-term relationship that wasn't bad, per se, but you didn't have an identity outside of it."

April groaned and dropped her face into her hands. "You make me sound like a cliché."

"If you're a cliché, then I'm a cliché." He waited until she raised her head before continuing. "I got married at twenty-five. High school sweetheart. We loved each other, but we got married more so because we thought it was what we were supposed to do. Had to do. And then time passed, and we started to grow apart. Had different ambitions and whatnot." He looked away for a split second, his jaw taut, until he turned back and said, "Eventually, we both realized we had no idea who we were outside of the relationship."

"I'm sorry," she whispered.

He waved her sympathy away. "The divorce was for the best. I don't regret it for a second. But all that to say I understand."

"I was headed down that path with my college sweetheart. In the end, I know I did the right thing when I broke it off. But there are still times when I'm..." She trailed off.

While she didn't want to use the word *lonely*—it felt like a betrayal to all the hard work she'd done on herself over the years—she wasn't sure how else to explain the level of detachment she had reached in her life. She had her family and her friends, but everyone was paired up. Everyone had someone to share memories with, spend time with, and build a future with. She was no one's first choice for anything.

And while she'd been able to fill that void with work and had met some nice people during her years on the road, all those connections were fleeting. Even this one would be. And that thought sobered her thoroughly.

Her eyes prickled with tears. Truthfully, she was overdue for a good cry, and mixing wine with hard liquor would do it. She rubbed her eyelids with her hands to hide the emotion on her face and joked, "Oh God, I've officially entered the drunken-confession portion of the night."

"Don't worry," he murmured, his stare tender. "Like I told you the other day, there's nothing I haven't heard in this line of work."

She sipped at her water, then went with self-deprecation. "Yeah, I bet you're used to pathetic women spilling their guts to you."

"You're not pathetic," he asserted firmly. "Honestly, life has a way of getting away from us, doesn't it?"

"That it does," she uttered in agreement.

"When I got divorced, I was certain I'd find someone new. I should have known better, considering I hadn't been on a first date since I was seventeen." He laughed and then cringed as if memories had rushed straight to the surface. "Christ, I was rusty."

She raised her glass to that and said, "Tell me about it."

Nick shrugged, and she desperately wanted to drape her arms across those broad shoulders. "I think we're doing okay right now."

His voice was low and intimate, and it sent heat straight to her core. Her heart rocketed against her rib cage, threatening to burst from her chest and right into his hands, when the barback, who April assumed was the aforementioned Jimmy, popped over to ask for assistance in the back room. Nick held up his index finger to her, signaling that he'd be a minute.

All alone, she took a deep breath. Should she proposition him or wait for him to take action? Should she slip him her extra keycard or wait for him to write down his number on a cocktail napkin? She knew what Lucy would tell her to do. It would certainly be an all-caps text message. Something like **BE DIRECT!** or **ASK WHEN HE GETS OFF AND IF HE WANTS TO GET OFF!**

But something held April back from making a move. And when Nick returned, bestowing her with an endearing smile—as if he was simply thrilled by the fact she was still there—the realization hit her square in the chest like a freight train.

She *liked* him. She actually, truly liked him. Her emotions were already involved, fully tangled up in him, and sex would only amplify those feelings. If she slept with him, there was no possibility of getting out of this unscathed. A vacation fling only worked if the memories were left where they were created. Considering how he already gave her butterflies and made her entire body heat like a furnace, there was no chance the memory of him would stay in Seattle. It would follow her back to New York and taunt her with what could never be.

"Listen...I have a few more things to finish up here," Nick started lightly. "And I know you've knocked a few more back than I have, but if you're up for a nightcap—"

"Yes," she blurted out before he could finish.

So much for self-preservation.

Once again, she slapped her hand over her mouth in embarrassment, but Nick was charmed at her eagerness, the smitten grin unmistakable. She smiled back timidly, under his spell completely by this point.

With a shaky hand, April reached for a cocktail napkin and pulled a pen out of her purse. She wrote her phone number down and pushed it toward him. "You can call me when you're done. Or text. Whatever you prefer."

He folded the napkin carefully, as if it was the most precious thing he'd ever held, and placed it in his back pocket. "I should only be twenty minutes, maybe a half hour at most."

Nodding, she rummaged around in her purse for a tip. She placed the dollar bills down on the bar, and they locked eyes, an unspoken communication in the air. Whatever had formed between them was destined to progress beyond the confines of this venue. They would no longer be the businesswoman and the bartender.

She slid off the stool and slung her purse over one shoulder. "See you in a bit, then."

Nick dipped his head in acknowledgment as she turned and left the lounge. The hotel's small grab-and-go market was on the path back to the elevator bay. She'd made a habit of stopping there for coffee every morning, but tonight she had her eye on something a bit harder. There was white wine and beer tucked away in the cooler, so she picked up a four-pack of IPA from a local brewery. After paying the cashier, she took the elevator up to her floor and returned to her room.

Once the beer was situated in the mini fridge, she attempted to settle her racing heart, to no avail. She couldn't recall the last time she'd experienced such a wide range of emotions, each more intense than the next. One second, she was nervous, and the next, she was aroused, then she was certain she was going to puke, and then her belly flipped with unfiltered happiness.

To distract herself, she tidied up the room. She lined up her shoes along one wall and retrieved the bra she'd tossed aside yesterday evening, placing it back in her luggage with the rest of her dirty laundry. The desk was a jumbled mess, littered with conference materials—her name badge, the printed program, and brochures and other handouts. She discarded the materials she knew she wasn't going to keep and then straightened what was left.

Before she knew it, her phone rang. The sound was loud and shrill, and she jumped at the piercing noise. The caller ID listed an unknown number with a Washington area code. Her hands trembled as she answered.

"Hello?"

"Hey. It's Nick."

"Oh, hi," she said breathlessly, as if she was surprised to hear from him. As if she hadn't been quietly obsessing the past thirty minutes.

"I'm officially off the clock. If you're still interested...?"

"I am! Yes, of course. Of course I am." She closed her eyes and shook her head, lamenting at how she couldn't play this cool for the life of her. Right as she opened her mouth to tell him what her room number was, she remembered that he couldn't access the hotel floors without a keycard. "Give me a second. I'll be right down."

She shoved her feet back into her sneakers in an ungraceful hurry, grabbed her keycard, and headed downstairs. The elevator took an eternity to get to her floor, but the journey down to the lobby happened in the blink of an eye.

When the elevator doors opened, Nick stood on the other side. They stared at each other, the anticipation so palpable she could barely breathe. And it was impossible to ignore that the entire moment was an exact replica of her dream.

FOUR

In truth, it was not like her dream.

Because instead of Nick confidently striding into the elevator and cupping her between her legs, they were so caught up in staring at each other as if they were the main characters in a daytime soap opera that the elevator doors began to close. She yelped and kicked her leg out to catch the door, while he did the same with his left arm.

It was comical at best, embarrassing at worst.

The doors bounced back open, and Nick stepped into the lift. They laughed together, an acknowledgment of the absurdity of that slapstick routine. She scanned her keycard and pressed the button for the twenty-eighth floor. And then the doors closed, leaving them alone. It was the first time there wasn't a bar between them, and something as simple as that felt shockingly intimate.

"Hi," she finally choked out.

If she thought he looked good before, he was positively lethal now. He still wore his uniform of black dress pants and white button-down, but he'd loosened the top two buttons and had rolled the sleeves up to expose his corded forearms, one of which was covered in tattoos. Minor changes that made him look like a whole different person and drove her faint at the sight of him.

"Hey. Sorry I took a while. I waited until the rest of my coworkers left so they wouldn't see me...you know..."

Panic flared to life. "Oh God. You're not going to get in trouble for this, are you?"

He shook his head. "No. Or I don't think so. At least as long as no one knows." Catching her eye, he spoke plainly. "Honestly? I don't even care."

Guilt invaded her gut when she realized how she'd put him in a rotten position. The man was willing to risk his job to spend more time with her, and she hadn't had the foresight to realize that fraternizing with a patron could land him in hot water.

But he was already in the lift, and they were already ascending, so she shook off the shame as best she could. "I'm not sure what you like to drink, but I got some beer from the minimarket downstairs."

"Thanks," he said with a grateful nod.

The elevator dinged as it reached her floor, and the doors opened with a whoosh. She led him down the hallway to her room with bated breath, and when she inserted her keycard, the sound of the lock clicking was like the roar of a cannon. The door opened, and she let him pass, watching as he took in the room.

"Wow. Fancy," he observed.

April closed the door and turned the deadbolt. "You mean the room?" She gestured to the mini fridge, encouraging him to help himself to a beer. When he cracked a can open and took a gulp, she continued. "You've never seen the rooms here?"

He gave her a droll look. "What, you think I hook up with all my customers?"

Her face heated to an unequivocal shade of crimson. He'd said what they'd been dancing around but had never given words to. She shook her head meekly in response and then grabbed a bottle of water, chugging half of it down. Secretly, she was over the moon that he didn't make a habit of doing this—that she was different, special in some way. But a part of her still felt like she was flailing in a vast ocean without a life jacket.

Nick sat in the chair by the desk, allowing her to sit on the bed alone. Presumably a conscious decision on his part, as if putting a bit of physical distance between them meant he wanted her to set the pace. She appreciated the gallant gesture, even though she wanted to crawl into his lap and grind down. He took another swig of beer, and she was momentarily hypnotized by how the muscles in his throat worked.

"For the record, I also don't, um...hook up with bartenders when I'm on the road," she offered pitifully.

Amusement rippled over his features. "That's good to hear."

"I do have a confession to make, though."

He blanched at the abrupt change in topic. "Okay?"

"I didn't have a client dinner tonight. I went to the Italian place around the corner by myself. I wanted to come to the bar, but I was..." She trailed off and mentally searched for the words before throwing her hands up in defeat. "Scared, I guess. Or embarrassed. Or both? Because you were already consuming my thoughts, and I'm fully aware it's insane that someone I've shared only a few conversations with could affect me so much. I figured it would be better if I just...stayed away."

She blew out a breath and avoided his gaze. God, what was even happening here? This was not how she'd expected their nightcap to start. She'd envisioned something similar to her dream—immediate groping and mouths battling. Not messy confessions and this awkward seating arrangement. The tension between them had built for days and been poised to explode. Yet here they were. Almost afraid to get physically close to one another.

"I spent the whole night worried I'd said something wrong yesterday," Nick eventually disclosed. His voice was low and soft. A balm to the visceral burns of her insecurity. "That maybe I'd gotten too real or whatever, telling you about my mom. I couldn't figure out why you hadn't shown up. And then I thought I'd imagined the whole thing."

Her eyes shot up to his, and the vulnerability drawn on his face made her want to hold him close and never let go. "You didn't imagine anything," she assured him.

He leaned back in the chair and inhaled deeply. Instead of answering, he took a few more gulps of beer and watched her attentively. His stare wandered down the length of her, lingering on her painfully hard nipples, which were all too noticeable through her thin T-shirt.

The bad news? The wine, gin gimlet, and countless cups of water she'd gulped down tonight were wreaking havoc on her bladder.

"Excuse me for a second," she said, getting to her feet.

Nick nodded. "Of course."

As she proceeded to the bathroom, she heard him toss the empty beer can into the nearby recycling bin. She closed the door and quickly used the facilities. While at the sink washing her hands, she glanced in the mirror. She looked...like she'd been working all day and had knocked back a few.

Despite all that, she still had her wits about her, so she reapplied her mascara and spread a bit of concealer under her eyes, topping her touch-up off with lip balm. She knew sex was a certainty at this point—he was in her hotel room, after all—but vanity held strong. After one final perusal in the mirror, she nodded firmly at herself. Once she stepped outside, she would officially make a move. No more of this blundering small talk.

April opened the door and found Nick standing on the other side, leaning against the wall. "Oh, hi. Do you need...?" She stepped out and gestured behind her to the restroom.

Quick as a flash, he grabbed her waist and spun her around. He pushed her back against the wall he'd been leaning against, and an ardent gasp escaped her throat. Feeling his hands on her after only a few innocent touches was almost too much to bear.

"Yes, I *need*," he growled before sealing his mouth to hers.

The kiss was perfect—fervid and searching and reverent and frantic, the ultimate culmination of nights of shameless flirting and tentative connection. His fingers dug into her hips, and she finally draped her arms over his broad shoulders, indulging in the feel of his physique. His mouth worked magic, moving his lips against her own, and she opened to allow his tongue full entry. She was no novice when it came to kissing, but this was on another level. It stripped her bare, and she suddenly couldn't imagine ever doing this with anyone other than him.

It was dizzying to finally be so close to him—to taste the hint of beer on his lips and inhale his scent. An alluring aroma of sandalwood and citrus wafted from him and intoxicated her further. This man was more potent than any cocktail she'd ever consumed.

He pulled away abruptly and rested his forehead against hers. "Shit. Sorry," he panted.

"What are you apologizing for?"

"Mauling you like that."

"Oh, sure. I'm absolutely scandalized," she teased. "How dare you."

He laughed huskily and brought his hands up to cradle the back of her head. "Can I take your hair down?" he murmured.

Something about the simple question made her heart tingle. It was so wholesome. As if they were young lovers frolicking on a moor during the nineteenth century, as opposed to two people in their midthirties who had loved and lost and made mistakes but still somehow found the strength to be vulnerable with each other.

She nodded shyly, and he plucked the bobby pins out, tossing them to the side. Soon enough, her hair fell around her shoulders, a bit tangled and messy, considering it had been coiled for hours. He gently ran his hands through the strands, and she heard his chest rumble.

"This hair of yours," he groaned, leaning in to nuzzle the tresses. "I spent hours thinking about doing this. Running my hands through it."

"Really?"

"Really." Then he clutched her backside. "Your ass is also fantastic," he admitted, his tone and expression lacking a hint of shame.

Flushing with happiness, she gave him a peck on the lips and said, "Watching your large hands work the pepper mill that first night had me all hot and bothered."

Nick threw his head back and howled with laughter.

She followed suit, and they stumbled from the foyer back over to the main area of the room, unable to keep their hands off each other. She worked at the buttons on his shirt, and he pulled at her blazer, tossing it to the side.

"What do you like?" he murmured against her mouth.

I like you, she almost whispered back. But instead, she hummed, "Hmm?"

"In bed. What do you like?"

April tried to remember if any man had ever asked such a question. Her first time with her ex had been following a frat party their junior year. They'd both been buzzed, and the sex had been spontaneous and admittedly lackluster, but they'd eventually figured out the physical aspect of their burgeoning relationship. Years later, after the breakup, she remained celibate for years, allowing herself time to mourn the end of her most substantial romantic relationship. Since then, she'd slept with two more people—a guy she'd casually dated for four months before realizing he bored her to tears, and a messy one-night stand with a friend of Lucy's fiancé after their engagement party.

"Oh, you know," she hedged. Slipping her sneakers off, she reached over to the bedside lamp and turned it down, shrouding the room in mood lighting.

"No, I don't know," he needled flirtatiously. "That's why I asked."

By this point, his shirt was completely unbuttoned, and she was rendered speechless by the sight of his bare chest. The tattoos on his left arm snaked all the way up over his shoulder and to his pectoral. A thin layer of brown hair covered his upper body, trailing down his abdominal muscles. He wasn't cut and sculpted like a male model, but he was solidly built and beautifully normal. Unable to resist, she skimmed her hands up his chest and guided the shirt all the way off.

Lust took control of her tongue. "I like a bit of good, old-fashioned roughness. Nothing crazy. Maybe a hair pull here and an ass slap there. Give me a thorough pounding and call me a slut once or twice if you're into that sort of thing, but then in the next breath, tell me how pretty I am and kiss me gently, you know?"

Oh my God, *why* was she like this? Before she could die of embarrassment, he cupped her face in his hands and gave her a look that made her knees weak.

"Oh, I do know." He leaned in and brushed his lips against her own. "And you're very pretty."

The soft and sensual timbre of his voice created a ripple of bliss in her belly. And that ripple grew into a wave of fervid anticipation when he untucked her T-shirt and pulled it over her head, his hands immediately moving to the button of her dress pants. Considering how she'd given up on this fantasy coming to fruition, her undergarments were mismatched and simple—a white bra and lavender thong that was frayed along the top hem. But Nick didn't appear to mind, because seeing her undressed pulled a deep hum from his throat, and he tilted her head, capturing her mouth once more.

She fumbled with the button of his trousers, and he moved to plant kisses down her neck, sucking against the skin enough to make her whimper. "I forgot to ask what you like," she said breathlessly.

"I like you," he answered, the reply simple and sure, and like he'd pulled it directly from her own mind.

Her eyes stung with tears, but she swallowed down the emotion. He was too busy removing his pants to notice her maudlin moment, and her aroused awareness returned when he stood before her in a pair of black briefs. She realized then that his lower body had been concealed, thanks to the bar he always stood behind, and she gawked at his muscular thighs, which were particularly impressive.

As was the stiff length straining against the fabric of his briefs.

"Did you...play football or something?" she asked, still eyeing his strapping legs.

"Rugby."

"Shit, that's hot."

He chuckled under his breath and guided her down onto the bed. His brawny body bearing down on hers made her mewl with lust, and his erection pressed against her left hip bone as they found a comfortable position lying horizontal across the expansive bed. Their mouths reconnected, and he ran his hands up and down her body as if desperate to touch every inch of her.

She hissed in pleasure when he grasped her breasts, massaging the flesh through the cotton of her bra. Then he muttered something that sounded like *fuck it* before he frantically slipped his hands behind her back. He pulled at the clasp, and April arched her body to help him undo the undergarment. Soon the bra was chucked aside, and he bent his head to lavish attention to her breasts.

But before he could, she stopped him, placing her hands against his shoulders to hold him still. "I just realized—do you have a condom?" she asked worriedly.

His eyebrows furrowed in thought, but then his expression loosened. "Yeah. In my wallet."

"Oh, thank God."

Her wheeze of laughter turned into a shameless moan when he clasped one nipple between his lips and pulled relentlessly. Sparks danced across her skin, starting at where he sucked and hurtling down to her wet core.

She was incredibly aroused but also desperately wanted to keep her cool, to appear worldly and unaffected by him. "You came prepared. You knew I was a sure thing, huh?"

"Far from it. I'm well aware that you're out of my league."

Unease slithered in, curbing the lust coursing through her veins. "I'm...what?" she breathed out.

One of his hands held both wrists above her head, and the other rubbed against her panties. Her hips bucked, and the stimulation was almost enough to distract her from his comment, but something—the fatalistic delivery, perhaps—kept her from discounting it completely. She attempted to sit up, and her change in demeanor did not go unnoticed. He released her wrists immediately and leaned back on his haunches.

April searched his face as she rested up on her forearms. "I'm not out of your league," she asserted in a bewildered manner.

One corner of his mouth curled ruefully. "Just an expression."

"Is it?" she murmured.

His throat worked, as if a million different answers wanted to escape, but he wouldn't allow it. Finally, he said, "April, let's just have a good time, yeah?"

"I don't know if I can have a good time if you're feeling..." She trailed off.

For one thing, she didn't want to put words in his mouth. For another, she recognized that it was hypocritical to admonish him when she'd acted similarly—calling herself pathetic and saying she was a sure thing. They disparaged themselves easily as if it was second nature to them both.

"What I'm feeling is very turned on," he declared, his voice husky and a deliberate strategy to squash the peculiarity that lingered.

Perhaps it was a defensive tactic to act as if they were both undeserving. Because when he leaned in to kiss her, the promise of heartbreak was in the action. But if they could cling to this counterfeit unworthiness, maybe the inevitable outcome would hurt a little less.

"I think you're perfect for me," she whispered against his lips, the truth of the matter winning out in the end.

And I wish things were different.

She left that part unsaid.

A wonderful sound of contentment rumbled from his chest, and the kiss went from hot to incendiary. Finally, he slid his fingers underneath the fabric of her panties. They groaned in tandem as he skimmed through her slick folds and finished the exploration with a firm press against her clit. With a deft touch, he rubbed careful circles against the swollen bud using his index and middle finger. Her pelvis tried to lift, searching for more, and he granted her wish when he pushed one finger into her pussy.

"Oh my God," she whimpered, breaking the kiss.

"Fuck. So wet." He straightened himself to look down at her and grasped one of her breasts with his free hand. "Christ."

Deep satisfaction surged at his inability to string proper sentences together, and that feeling was compounded by his finger pumping in and out of her. There was something deliciously erotic about how he worked her with his hand while she still wore her thong. But eventually, he growled with impatience and pulled the piece of cotton off her body.

She hadn't had a wax appointment in ages, but her

unkempt state down below didn't faze him, because his eyes flashed with hunger as his hand returned to her core. This time two fingers pushed into her heat, thrusting steadily as his thumb played with her clit.

"I can't believe how wet you are," he gritted out between his teeth.

She was able to joke despite the searing passion. "Several nights of unintended foreplay will do that to a girl."

His laugh was devilish. "Well, it's hot as fuck. *You're* hot as fuck. Shit."

Nick slid off the side of the bed and kneeled on the floor. With a firm grasp on her hips, he pulled her body closer, and she cried out when he leaned down and latched his lips around her clit, sucking deep. She squirmed and panted and turned herself over to the feel of his mouth on her most intimate place.

Oh God, she couldn't care less that she was certain to get hurt when this was all over. All she could think about was how his tongue expertly lapped alongside the thrust of his fingers, coaxing forward the pleasure that had coiled within her body. Her legs were draped over his broad shoulders, and she dug her heels into his muscular back.

"*Nick*," she moaned, her voice almost unrecognizable it was so laced with lust. "Oh God, oh my God. Please, please."

His reply was muffled. "Hearing you beg is so fucking sexy."

"Is that what you want? For me to beg?"

Although his fingers didn't cease moving, he crept up her body until they were face to face. "I want a lot of things, April," he whispered.

Her heart was beating a mile a minute, but it stuttered

slightly at that quiet confession. Before she could unpack his true message, Nick flipped her onto her stomach and pushed her forward slightly to bring her lower body back onto the bed. Then the palm of his hand came down her bottom, the slapping sound reverberating throughout the room. She keened as a flood of wetness rushed between her legs.

He gently rubbed her stinging flesh and leaned over her. One side of her face rested on the bed, and he kissed the side facing him before he murmured, "How's that for a bit of good, old-fashioned roughness?"

She chuckled and nodded her approval against the mattress.

"Do you know how hard it was to watch you walk away from the bar last night?" he grunted in her ear as he stroked her hair. "Your face was all flush and pretty, and then you turned away from me, and I only had a few seconds to savor you. To watch this ass of yours in those tight pants as you left. The memory of it kept me up all night."

Another smack came down, this time on the other cheek. It felt so good, she could barely stand it. She gulped air and trembled, trying to construct a sexy comeback. Instead, she huffed out a breath in wonder and said, "I can't believe we're doing this."

He flipped her back over abruptly and caught her gaze, once again giving her that look. As if his main purpose in life was to stare and drink her in, even if civilization itself was ending outside the doors of this room.

"I can't either," he said in a hushed tone.

He quickly stood and reached down to grab his wallet from the pocket of his trousers. When he tossed the square foil down on the bed, she reached forward and gripped his erection through the briefs. His hips jerked, and his breath caught as she lightly squeezed the firm bulge.

"Take these off," she ordered. "Now."

With a tiny laugh, he followed her command. He pushed the black cotton down his thighs, and his cock sprang free, a firm column of flesh surrounded by a nest of light-brown hair. She wanted nothing more than to get her mouth around it, so she rose onto her knees and moved into the center of the bed. She crooked a finger at him, intending to get him properly positioned.

A suggestive smile lit up his face as he shifted onto the mattress and advanced toward her, but she pushed him to sit back against the headboard. His sturdy legs spread open, and she kneeled between them, watching as he spit in his hand and used the natural lubricant to stroke his cock. The blatantly sexual display made her burn all over, and she trailed her hands up his thighs, pressing her nails into his skin.

"Let me." She looked at him pointedly and then bent low.

Her intention was unmistakable, and he breathed raggedly when she removed his hand and placed it on the back of her head. And then she took him in her mouth, closing her lips around the thickness. He swore vehemently, and then his hand clenched and tangled in her hair. But he allowed her to set the pace, and she bobbed her head up and down, sucking and licking and enjoying the intimate act.

And, because she was shameless and already knew what he liked, she shifted slightly, bringing her tits closer to the mattress and arching her back even more. The change in position made her ass jut up for his viewing enjoyment.

"Ah, fuck," he cursed when he saw what she'd done. He

carefully leaned forward and grasped both cheeks with his hands, squeezing roughly, before he fell back against the headboard. "You're trying to kill me."

She grasped his shaft with one hand and rose up to meet his eyes. "You want me to stop?" she asked coyly.

"Never," he panted, his eyes rolling back as she pumped him steadily. Then he refocused and gripped her jaw with one hand. "Take me as deep as you can. And then I'm going to fuck you senseless."

Her inner muscles contracted at that promise, so she crouched down to take him back in her mouth. She breathed through her nose and relaxed her throat, taking his cock as far down as she could. Both of her hands rested on his thighs, and she felt his limbs shaking. He let loose a string of curse words that had her belly churning with heat.

"Enough." He guided her head up and kissed her like a madman, pulling her close. "Goddamn, you're incredible. I need you. Right now, before I lose it."

Both were near to bursting when he tore the condom packet open. His hands were unsteady as he rolled the latex over his pulsing shaft, then shifted so she could straddle him.

She gradually sank down onto his cock with a gasp, her eyes fluttering. Although she was beyond wet, she went slowly, adjusting to how he stretched her. When fully seated, she opened her eyes and found his stormy gaze. His jaw clenched, and his chest rose unevenly, but he never once looked away from her.

"Good?" he whispered.

Her head bobbed in agreement. "So good."

One hand smacked her ass. "Then show me what you've got."

A burst of aroused laughter left her lips, but then she

rose and pressed down once more, and the laughter was gone. All that was left were whimpers and moans and pleasure-filled cries as she rode him. His large hands clutched her bottom and helped her move, establishing a rocking rhythm that had her unable to think straight. She dug her fingers into his pectorals as the pressure built.

Her eyes fluttered closed often, passion overtaking her, but each time she refocused her attention, she found him watching her as if she were a dream.

When her climax was imminent, she rubbed her clit with determined strokes. Her cadence faltered, and he noticed immediately. He held her hips in place and thrust up steadily, allowing her to focus on the movement of her fingers. Soon enough, her body stiffened as the first burst of sensation hit, followed by delicious pulses that laid her bare.

Her cries echoed throughout the room, and she distantly heard Nick's voice. She wished she could decipher what he'd said, but the orgasm had complete control over her senses. Eventually, she wilted, but before she collapsed against him, he flipped her onto her back. He lifted her lower body, grabbed one of the numerous pillows on the bed, and wedged it under her pelvis. Her legs naturally hitched back as he braced himself up on his hands to watch her.

"Oh God," she whimpered, still in and out of a rapturous daze. Her inner muscles continued to clench every now and then—tiny throbs that were all the more delicious when he plunged deep, thanks to their new position and the angle the pillow created.

"That was hot as hell," he said, his voice layered with gravel. "Seeing you lose control like that? Shit. I nearly came from how tight you squeezed my cock."

"Why didn't you?" she asked. All she wanted now was

for him to reach his own finish—to feel as satisfied as she did.

"Because I'm not fucking done with you yet."

He had promised to fuck her senseless and did just that. His thrusts picked up speed, their hips smacking together to create the most lewd and wonderful sound. As his body worked and worshipped hers, he kissed her over and over, as if frightened he'd never be able to do it again. His mouth moved down to her neck, and he dragged his teeth lightly against her skin before sucking hard.

She clutched his back, loving the feel of his taut muscles underneath her fingers. But she loved it even more when he grabbed her arms and pinned her wrists above her head.

"Oh, fuck," she groaned, feeling helpless but still taken care of.

"Let me hear it. Get loud and dirty for me."

"Don't stop," she panted. "I've wanted this for days. Don't fucking stop."

One eyebrow raised, and the smile on his face was pure sex. "Days, huh?"

"Since the moment I saw you."

He groaned and hunched down to kiss her. "Me too. God, I wanted you so bad."

"You have me. So don't stop fucking me."

With a raunchy laugh, he obeyed. Somehow, another orgasm emerged, starting low in her belly, then exploding like a firecracker. Her moans were continuous as he fucked her through the second bout of pleasure. Soon after, his movements became erratic, and his grip on her wrists tightened harshly.

"Oh, fuck. April. Fuck," he boomed. "Shit, I'm gonna come."

A primal growl pealed through the room as his climax

erupted, his body jerking as he finished inside the condom. They fought for breath in unison as the euphoric moment unfurled.

"No one has ever—oh God, April—that was—"

"I know," she agreed, knowing exactly what he was thinking.

No one has ever made me feel like this before. That was incredible.

Once their breathing stabilized, Nick carefully pulled out, minding the condom. "Give me a second," he rasped.

She nodded shakily, utterly spent as he advanced toward the bathroom to deal with the condom's disposal. He returned a moment later and knelt on the mattress, resting down beside her. Gently, he took her wrists and kissed the inside of each as if to ward off the inevitable bruises. But she wanted those marks—wanted to see the proof of tonight on her skin.

"What do you need?" he asked. "I can run you a shower, or a bath, maybe?"

Shaking her head, she skimmed one hand over his cheek, wishing she could see him with a beard. "Spend the night?"

That was what she needed. And fortunately, he smiled and murmured, "Of course."

Sometime later, she was able to get to her feet and made it to the restroom on wobbly legs. She headed to the toilet first to relieve herself, then washed her hands and tended to her before-bed routine—makeup removal, face wash, moisturizer, toothbrush, floss, and mouthwash.

Nick was right where she'd left him, sprawled out on the top of the comforter, gloriously naked. She approached him tentatively, conscious of her own nakedness and makeup-free face, and still somehow worried that he was an illusion. That everything that had happened tonight was only another dream, this one more vivid than her prior fantasy.

"I don't have an extra toothbrush, but there's plenty of mouthwash if you want," she offered.

"Thanks. Let's get you into bed. I'll be back in a minute."

He stood and pulled back the comforter for her, and she climbed onto the mattress, settling under the crisp sheets. Before heading to the bathroom, he turned the light down completely to blanket them in total darkness. Languor crept in as she waited for him, her eyes fluttering closed.

After a short time, the bed dipped as he joined her. "You still awake?" he whispered.

"A little," she answered, which amused him.

He stretched out like a jungle cat with a resounding sigh. Then he pulled her close, and she rested her head on his chest. Exhaustion clung to her, but she didn't want to go to sleep. Sleeping meant losing precious time with him, and the last thing she had was time.

"Nick?"

"Hmm?"

"What's your last name?" she asked, the words drowsy.

"Daniels. What's yours?"

"Markham."

"April Markham," he mused, lightly tracing his fingers up and down her arm. "I'm glad I met you, April Markham."

She hummed a sound of harmony and then sighed. "That was...amazing."

He kissed the top of her head. "The best."

Contentment filled her at his agreement. Despite her serious effort to stay awake and talk with him until the sun came up, she was lulled into sleep. Her heart had steadied in the time following their coupling, but there was a tiny twinge that remained—one she couldn't ignore.

To think she assumed jet lag would be the biggest challenge to contend with during this trip. That was child's play compared to the thought of leaving him behind.

FIVE

It had been ages since she'd shared a bed with a man. All of the sensations—the sound of heavy breathing, the crisp hair on his legs rubbing her bare skin, the rustling of his body against the bedsheets—felt foreign but, at the same time, were so welcome. At some point during the night, she was pulled from sleep by his lethargic kisses. Easy and exquisite kisses that she was all too happy to partake in despite being half-awake. And then, as quickly as they'd started, he stopped and nuzzled against her. They fell back asleep, tangled up in one another.

Her alarm sounded at seven. She swung out her arm sleepily and grasped her phone to silence the piercing sound.

Nick pulled her closer and murmured, "What time?"

"Seven." She adored how physically affectionate he was. How he unabashedly enjoyed a good cuddle. Their bodies fit so well together, and it made the prospect of leaving the bed unfathomable.

"Ugh."

April giggled at his distaste for the early hour. "When do you have to be at work?"

As soon as the question left her mouth, she worried the reemergence of his job would make things awkward. Try as they might, there was no way to stop reality from filtering back in.

"Three," he answered. "I'll head to my place soon to grab a shower and a change of clothes. Even though I wear the same thing every day."

She smiled and lifted her head to glance around the room. "Your pants are around here somewhere. But I imagine your shirt is wrinkled beyond belief."

He grinned. "Worth it."

A muscular arm curved around her body, and his hand lazily grasped her left breast, tweaking the hard nipple. With a wistful sigh, she asked, "You only brought one condom?"

Nick burrowed his head into the crook of her neck and grumbled. "Rookie mistake. I'll bring a bunch tonight." He paused, and she felt his body tense. "That is, if you want to do this again?"

She raised up onto her forearm to look down at him. "Of course. Would it be too weird if I come to the bar? I don't want anyone getting suspicious or anything."

He considered that. "I think a nightcap would be safest. If you're there the whole night, I doubt I'll keep my cool."

Grinning, she swung one leg over his body and straddled him. "Nor could I."

Kissing ensued. Lots and lots of kissing. So much so that Nick stopped them with a remorseful look on his face. "I *really* regret not bringing more condoms."

April giggled once more and climbed off the bed, grabbing his hand and pulling him to his feet. His erection jutted out, thick and ready for action. Eyeing it eagerly, she led him to the bathroom. "We can still have fun."

Fun consisted of a steaming shower and her on her knees, sucking him eagerly, followed by his large fingers plunging between her legs. By eight o'clock, they were fully showered and satiated. April dressed in jeans and a gray turtleneck—which she was thankful she'd had the foresight to pack since there was a visible hickey on her neck—whereas Nick stepped into his crumpled clothes from the night before. They sat on the bed, and she laced up her sneakers while he tended to his own shoes.

"What time are you going to the Needle?" he asked.

"I was planning to get there right when they open. And, if I have time afterward, maybe walk around that glass thing?"

"Chihuly Garden and Glass," he supplied with a tiny smile.

"Yes, that. And then my boat tour is at noon."

"What are you doing for lunch?"

"Probably explore the market, see what I'm in the mood for."

He ran his hands up and down his thighs once, then twice, as if summoning his nerve. "Do you think you'd want company?"

Every inch of her vibrated with joy. "I'd love that. I should be off the boat by one o'clock. Want to meet me then?"

"Sounds like a plan."

"What about breakfast? Can you join me before you head back to your place?"

Nick knew of a bakery about ten minutes away. He left first and told her he'd wait at the corner two blocks down. April remained in the room for a full five minutes before departing, feeling like a teenager sneaking out of her house after hours. She met him on the corner, right where he said he'd be, and they proceeded to the bakery.

The space was intimate and cozy, with a handful of circular tables, counter service, and a display case that held every pastry under the sun—each one more mouthwatering than the next. She ordered a small coffee and an almond croissant, and Nick followed suit. Before she could even open her purse, he handed over some bills to the cashier.

"Thank you," she said, giving his arm a squeeze of gratitude.

He smiled ruefully. "Don't thank me. That was your money anyway." When her brows knit with confusion, he clarified, "The tip you left last night?"

"Oh." She laughed lightly. Yet nothing felt funny, especially not when a memory resurfaced.

I'm well aware that you're out of my league.

Luckily, the fraught moment passed, and their conversation over breakfast was easy and natural. Topics ranged from the basic, like their families—he had three older sisters; she had a younger brother—to the absurdly specific, like whether they believed in ghosts or not. They were thrilled to find out they were both total believers.

After the pastries and coffee were consumed, they went their separate ways. But before Nick jumped on the light rail bound for his neighborhood, he kissed her easily, in the way that proper couples do. It made her stomach twist and turn with equal parts elation and terror.

She spent the rest of the morning on her feet, exploring Seattle—the breathless height of the Space Needle, the brilliant artistry of Chihuly Garden and Glass, and the sereneness of Elliott Bay. It was a clear and crisp day, and she felt more alive than she'd felt in a long, long time. And that feeling was only amplified when she stepped off the boat later that afternoon and found Nick waiting for her.

They headed from the water up to Pike Place Market, which was a feast for the eyes and evoked all the senses. They walked past the different vendors and artisans, purchasing bits of food as they went, and April bought a stunning hand-painted scarf for her mother's birthday next month.

And, at the end of the day, she was a tourist, so she begged him to show her where they threw the fish. She clapped happily as the workers tossed a gigantic salmon through the air and called out orders, and Nick watched her with tender eyes. She hoped that he found joy in how *she* found joy in his city.

Throughout the afternoon, they peppered each other with question after question, eager to find out as much as they could. Most of the inquiries were basic—favorite color, first kiss, most embarrassing moment. But after they gorged on mac and cheese at Beecher's and returned to wandering the street, April dug deeper and asked, "What are you most proud of?"

He appeared genuinely stumped for a second, and then his reply was hesitant. "You'll probably think it's silly."

"If you're proud of it, then it's not silly."

Nick turned his head to search her eyes as if he couldn't trust the sincerity in her voice. But he eventually said, "I was voted best bartender in Seattle a few years back."

She stopped dead in her tracks and playfully whacked him on the arm. "Are you kidding me? That's amazing!"

"It was just a little online blog thing, not a big deal—"

"It is a big deal. Many people aren't recognized for their work. The fact that you were is incredible. And I happen to agree. You *are* the best bartender in Seattle," she added cheekily, raising onto her tiptoes to kiss his cheek.

One skeptical eyebrow raised in response. "And how many bartenders in this city do you actually know?"

"Doesn't matter," she insisted with an impish grin. "You're the best, and I won't hear otherwise."

A sheepish laugh bubbled from his throat as he took her hand, lacing their fingers together so easily she almost cried. How unfair it was that he lived here while she lived thousands of miles away. She would give anything to bottle this moment up and relive it any time she wanted.

At two thirty, he regretfully announced that he had to leave to make his shift on time. She promised to come by around ten for a quick nightcap, and, after a goodbye kiss, he was off.

April spent another half hour at the market, browsing through a used bookstore. She stopped at the original Starbucks for a coffee, then strolled back to her hotel. As she did, she received another text from Lucy.

Did the bone happen? I'm dying here.

She giggled and replied:

Yes. It was amazing, and he's great. I'll call you tomorrow after I land. You can interrogate me then.

Lucy sent back a bunch of celebratory emoji and a few eggplants for good measure.

Because it was still too early for dinner, April returned to her room and took a quick nap. Her legs ached from all the walking, albeit in the most pleasant way. Not to mention the other parts of her body that ached, which she savored wholeheartedly.

When they'd been down at the water, Nick had pointed out a restaurant he'd worked at previously, so she went there for dinner later that evening and indulged in Dungeness crab legs with a roasted veggie medley. After a satisfying meal, she stopped by her hotel room to touch up her makeup and, when the clock approached ten, headed downstairs.

And there he was, standing behind the bar, slinging drinks and looking exactly as he had the first night she'd laid eyes on him. Except nothing was the same. Not for her.

The bar was almost full, but she found a seat between two middle-aged men. Nick approached as if she was any other customer and placed a cocktail napkin down on the bar. "Evening."

It was difficult to hide a coy smile, but April succeeded. "Evening. I'll have an old fashioned."

He balked and then tilted his head to the side, silently asking if she'd lost her mind. She giggled, unable to commit to the joke for long.

"Kidding," she said. "I'll have my usual. You know what I like."

"That I do," he purred suggestively.

Mercifully, it was too loud and crowded for anyone to overhear, but her face still heated blatantly, and liquid pooled between her legs. However, a busy night meant Nick wasn't able to lavish attention on her, which worked in their favor. She got her libido under control and enjoyed her favorite cocktail made by her new favorite person, while he focused on his job, and no one was any the wiser of what had transpired between them the night before.

The one downside to being a single woman sitting at a

bar? Men often took it as an invitation to converse. When she'd claimed her stool, both men she'd sat between wore wedding rings. But when the man to her right attempted to chat her up a few minutes later, his ring was mysteriously missing, no doubt hastily stuffed in his pocket. Nevertheless, she chose politeness and endured the mindless chitchat. It was a chore to not roll her eyes at his inflated ego —how he was allegedly the most successful real estate agent in the region and had recently returned from a trip to Santorini—but she somehow managed.

Last call was announced at eleven, and the nuisance to her right leaned in and suggested they grab another drink at the pub across the street.

"Thanks, but I'm taken," she told him with a short smile. It was almost a force of habit to use that lie to rebuff unwanted invitations from men. But this was the first time it felt *real*.

And speak of the devil. The object of her affection drifted over and asked if she wanted a final drink, but she declined and asked to settle the bill.

"Put it on my tab," the man said to Nick, not even bothering to look his way.

Nick raised one eyebrow at her in question. Despite how his mouth curled, hints of worry flashed in his expression.

The eye roll she'd been suppressing for nearly an hour finally won out, which appeared to calm him. "That's not necessary," she told the man in the firmest voice she could muster. She handed her credit card to Nick without even asking to review the check.

The man next to her took care of his bill as well before thankfully making a quick exit. After the final sip of her gimlet, she pushed the check holder back toward Nick with a reassuring smile. It contained more than a signed receipt and cash tip—her extra keycard was hidden beneath. As she stepped down from the stool, she peered at him as he deftly slipped the cash and card into his pocket.

He turned to look over his shoulder and met her eyes. Carnal heat swirled in his gaze, but something else was layered into the stare that she couldn't pinpoint—something tumultuous or troubled—and it stopped her in her tracks.

But then his face softened, and he nodded gingerly, a clear communication that he'd see her again shortly.

Back in her room, she dozed on the bed for a bit and lost track of time. Then she heard the click of the door unlocking, and she jumped up to skip over to the entranceway. The door closed behind him with a slam, and he pinned her with a steady, intent look that sent an electrifying chill down her spine.

"Welcome back," she greeted softly, taking a few steps closer.

His hand shot out and cupped between her legs, pushing his fingers against the denim. Gasping with the memory of her dream blaring in her mind, she rose onto her tiptoes due to the force of his grip. He pressed her back against the wall and raised his other hand up to eye level.

Between his index and middle finger was the folded-up ten-dollar bill she'd left alongside the keycard. It was an excessive amount for only one cocktail, but she knew that those working in the food and beverage industry depended on tips, and she assumed he was no different. He deserved to be compensated for his hard work, but it hadn't occurred to her the impression a tip would leave after they'd slept together.

He pushed the bill into her front pocket and said, "I don't want your money."

"But you—"

"I what? Earned it?"

Her stomach flipped over viciously. "That's not what I was going to say," she whispered.

His features eased, and he bowed his head, resting it gently against her brow. "I know it's not," he said on a shaky exhale. "But I just—I don't—"

Unable to find the words, he paused, and his body sagged in the silence. When his hand fell away from between her thighs, she grabbed his wrist and placed it back there, right where it belonged. A rumble vibrated from his chest, like the distant sound of thunder, and his frame straightened.

"I just want *you*, okay?" he said, voice hoarse with emotion.

Nodding, she pressed her lips to his tentatively. "I understand."

He turned her cautious kiss into one of pure obsession, pushing his erection against her belly. His hands snared her hips roughly, and April knew this coupling wouldn't be soft and sweet. No, it was destined to be wild and angry because it was their last night together, and she couldn't allow it to be romantic.

"Fuck me from behind. Right here," she implored, snapping open the button of her jeans and pulling down the zipper. "Bend me over and fuck me."

He whipped her around with a guttural groan, and she planted her hands against the wall. With a ferocious shove, he dragged her jeans and panties to bunch around her thighs. Moisture flooded her core when he pressed one hand between her shoulder blades, forcing her back to arch. She was on display for him, and it made her tremble with need.

Facing the wall, she was at the mercy of only a few senses. His belt clanked as he unbuckled it, and then the rip of the condom packet filled the space, both noises mixing with her already labored breathing. He swiped two fingers through her pussy to make sure she was wet enough, and then he shoved his cock home.

She cried out and dug her nails into the wall, wishing it was the flesh of his back. The restriction of her jeans meant her legs were fixed together, providing a delicious tightness as he drilled deep, his hands gripping her ribcage. She pushed back onto his cock, slapping her bottom against his groin, and curved her back even more once she established a tempo.

"God, that is fucking filthy," he praised. "Keep doing that. Let me see that ass move."

She heeded his instructions and continued to launch her hips back, relishing the intense penetration. "Pull my hair," she pleaded.

"Yeah?" One hand coiled around her locks and tugged, jerking her head back until his lips brushed her ear as he whispered, "Does my slutty little barfly like that?"

Acute lust barreled through her, and she almost came on the spot at the crude question. "Yes," she moaned. "Don't stop."

He didn't stop. He fucked her so hard that her vision blurred. "You think that douchebag at the bar could hit you this deep?"

It took her a few moments to register who he had referred to. If she wasn't a complete prisoner to her arousal, she would have laughed at the prospect that she had eyes for anyone other than him. But she shook her head and choked out, "No."

"What's that?" he pressed pointedly, pulling at her hair harder.

"No!" Her passionate plea turned into a jumble of nonsensical words and phrases. "Just you—only you, okay? Only—oh, God. Nick, I don't—I don't want anyone other than you. Anything other than this."

"You're so incredible. God, you're so fucking incredible," he chanted. "And this pussy is so tight, I can't fucking handle it."

The intensity increased, and his free hand wrapped around her body to find her clit. One press of his index finger ruptured her control, her entire body shaking and trembling as pleasure took over. She came with sobs and screams and would have fallen to the floor if he hadn't released her hair and wrapped both arms around her body.

"Oh my God. *Oh my God*," she cried.

It took a few moments, but she recovered as much as possible. She tried to reestablish her prior movement to meet his strokes, but he held her hips firm with both hands and railed her like a man possessed.

"I want to come all over this ass of yours," he grunted. "Coat your pretty skin with it."

Her pussy responded to his words, and if his primal groan was any indication, he felt the contraction all too well. "Yes," she gasped out. "Do it. Please. Nick, please."

With a tormented snarl, he pulled out and tossed the condom off to the side. She stayed in position but craned her head to watch as he stroked his swollen cock in search of his peak. His free hand clutched one of her ass cheeks as his hips bucked, and his release thundered through him, thick streaks spurting onto her flesh.

"Oh, *fuck me*," he bellowed, still twitching with the aftershocks of ecstasy. "April—fuck—are you—?"

"Yes," she breathed out, already knowing what he'd sought to ask. "I'm okay."

He rested his forehead against her back. "Are you sure?"

"Well...I'm not sure I can walk after that. But yeah, I'm great."

Huffing a laugh, he curled around to kiss her. "Don't move."

He took a few steps to the bathroom and returned with a damp washcloth, which he used to clean her coated skin. Then he pulled her jeans all the way down and carefully helped her step out of them. Her shirt was removed next, and he carried her the short distance into the restroom, where he ran a bath in the luxurious tub.

He held her hand as she shakily stepped over the ledge and settled in the heated water. She didn't have to coax him to join her, since he immediately shed his clothes and positioned himself behind her, the water sloshing around them. They sat in satiated silence, but a million thoughts roared through her brain.

We're good together, aren't we?

I'm not crazy for thinking there's something here, right?

Would you want to visit New York sometime?

Should we maybe give this a try?

But she never voiced any of them, and soon their skin pruned. They left the tub and toweled off, retiring to bed.

She slept restlessly, as if her body sensed that she shouldn't waste any of the time she had left with him. And he seemed to have the same thought because, at some point in the dead of night, he fumbled for his wallet and retrieved another condom. Her eyesight had adjusted to the dark, so she saw the question in his eyes and nodded her consent.

They quietly moved and rocked against each other in

soft lovemaking that was the opposite of their earlier frenzied fucking. And yet, it suited them just as well.

SIX

She'd never wanted to miss a flight more in her life.

It was early morning, and she still hadn't packed. As a frequent traveler, she'd established a strict routine over the years—the night before the flight, she laid out her travel clothes, which often consisted of leggings and a sweatshirt, and packed everything but her toiletries. Then the next morning, she collected the final pieces, placed them in her luggage, and was on her way. Clean, easy, and straightforward.

But departing Seattle would be none of those things.

They were still tangled up in bed when Nick whispered, "What time is your flight?"

"Eleven."

He lifted his head to find the digital clock on the nightstand, and then his chest lifted and fell with a despondent sigh. "We should start getting up."

"We should," she agreed glumly. "But I don't want to."

"I know." He paused and kissed her temple. His lips lingered there as he pulled in a breath. "Trust me, I know."

Nevertheless, they eventually schlepped out of bed and

dressed. She packed in silence, and Nick assisted when he could, placing the cap on her toothpaste and checking the room to make sure she'd unplugged all her chargers from the outlets. The entire process was exceedingly morose, like a funeral for a relationship that had never fully begun.

If nothing else, she promised herself she wouldn't cry in front of him. She'd wait until they finally parted ways, and then she'd allow the tears to fall. It was certain to be a wretched six-hour flight back east, but she'd survive it somehow. And while she was proud of herself for finally opening her heart again, she would give anything to have more time with him.

He sat on the bed and watched as she kneeled on the floor to zip her luggage. She didn't want to look at him—it would make her cry prematurely. But at the same time, all she wanted was to stare at his face and commit him to memory, to keep him in the secret and sacred place she rarely allowed anyone to go.

Out of the blue, he spoke and shattered the silence. "I have a buddy who lives in Queens."

Time stood still as she took in his words. Then she turned her head to look at him. "You what?"

He nodded slowly. There was uncertainty in his features, and his eyes searched hers intensely before he said, "An old high school friend. He moved out there for work a few years back. I've been thinking it might be nice to visit."

The knot that had formed in her chest over the past few days started to dissipate thread by thread. "Is that right?"

"You don't suppose you'd want to...maybe..."

She launched herself at him, enveloping him in a hug. They fell back onto the bed together, and she buried her face in the crook of his shoulder as emotion rushed to the surface.

Despite her attempt to conceal the waterworks, he caught on. "Oh God, I don't want you to cry."

"I'm crying because I'm happy," she insisted. "Why didn't you tell me this earlier?"

"Because I wasn't sure what this was. Hell, I'm still not even sure—"

"Neither am I. But it's something, right?"

He cradled her head, tilted it back, and softly grazed her lips. "It's something."

They lay together on the bed for some time, fully clothed but content. Or so she thought.

"You sure you want to get into a situationship with a bartender who lives across the country?" he asked, the question much too defeated for her liking.

I'm well aware that you're out of my league.

April rose onto one elbow. "Nick, do you like what you do?"

He blinked, and his brow tightened as if surprised by her question. But then the confusion alleviated, and he nodded. "I do, yeah. I always have. But sometimes, it feels like people look at me and wonder why I didn't pursue something different. Something better, more meaningful."

"People like your ex?"

There was a lengthy pause before he finally said, "Maybe."

The idea that someone he loved would judge him for a career he enjoyed and excelled at irritated April to no end. But she shoved the annoyance down to reassure him.

"All work is honorable work, so long as you're not hurting anyone," she said. "My dad is a line cook in a local restaurant. My mom's a hairdresser."

"Really?"

She nodded steadily. "I might seem fancy, but I wasn't

raised that way. You don't have to worry about any of that, okay? As long as you're happy with your career, then I'm happy."

The worry that clouded his face gradually eased. He clasped her hand and kissed her knuckles. It appeared as if he wanted to speak but couldn't find the words, so she squeezed his hand to convey that he didn't need to say anything. She wasn't foolish enough to believe that only a few words from her would erase all his insecurities, but it was the truth, and it was a start.

"How are you getting to the airport? Car?" he asked, switching topics.

"Yeah, I can expense it."

Nick saw to her luggage, throwing her backpack over his shoulder and grasping the handle of her roller bag. "I'll ride with you. I can take the Link back. The light rail," he clarified when he saw her confused look. "It goes to Sea-Tac."

"That's not out of your way?"

"Not for you, it's not."

They proceeded down to the first floor and stepped outside the hotel, lingering under the overhang. It was raining lightly, the climate most associated with Seattle. April had been blessed with sunny skies throughout her trip, but she wished she could stay and experience some quintessential Pacific Northwest weather.

However, the car arrived quickly and squashed that dream. Nick helped haul her luggage into the trunk, and then they both settled into the backseat as the driver began the journey to the airport. Their hands were laced together and situated comfortably on his thigh, while her head rested on his shoulder. The car ride was silent. There was still so much to say, but not enough time to say it.

The ride to Sea-Tac happened in the blink of an eye,

and before she knew it, the driver pulled up to the departure level at the airport. Still bereft of speech, they exited the car and retrieved her luggage before entering the building. She checked her bags and then turned to Nick.

"I guess this is it," she said somberly.

He pulled her into a powerful hug. "For now."

"For now," she repeated on a quivery breath, holding him tight.

The embrace turned into a poignant and passionate kiss. Not a goodbye kiss, but a tentative promise of things to come.

"Text me when you land, okay?" he said.

She agreed with a nod of her head, squeezed his hand, and made her way to security. She only turned to wave once, because if she looked back over her shoulder again, she'd likely never leave. He waved back with an encouraging smile, and soon she was through TSA and unable to see him.

As she stood in line to grab a coffee and pastry at one of the airport's cafés, her phone buzzed.

> Have a safe flight. Talk to you in a few hours.

The message, as simple as it was, meant everything. It was proof she hadn't imagined the entire affair, and that he would remain in her life despite the distance between them. She didn't know what the future held, but the pressure in her chest eased when she typed out a reply.

> Thank you. Talk to you tonight. XOXO.

She sipped at her coffee, devoured her pastry, and made

her way to the gate, counting down the minutes until she could speak to him again.

And miraculously, not one tear was shed on her flight back to New York.

THREE MONTHS LATER, April stood near baggage claim at JFK, nearly jumping up and down with excitement like a kid on the last day of school. Dozens of people had come down the escalator since she'd arrived, but she still waited for a special someone.

After a few moments, she spotted him, and fierce happiness swept through her like wildfire. He descended the escalator wearing jeans, a flannel shirt, and a bomber jacket. The complete antithesis of his work uniform, but she would recognize him anywhere. His eyes combed the crowd, and a radiant smile appeared when he spotted her.

She dashed around groups of people to make her way toward him. He got a few steps away from the bottom of the escalator before she attacked him with a hug, and he lifted her off her feet.

"Finally," she breathed, more to herself than to him.

Laughing, Nick squeezed her tight and then placed her back on the ground to grant her a proper kiss. "Hi," he greeted her softly.

"Hi." She ran her hands over his cheeks, caressing the faint stubble and the crescents that bracketed his mouth. "This is nice."

"Figured I'd grow it out while I'm here."

"I love that idea."

Since leaving Seattle, their relationship had flourished over the phone. She received a text message from him each morning —everything from *Good morning, beautiful* to *I dreamed about you all night, and now I'm hard as fuck.* They carved out time for a phone call every day, usually before he started his nightly shift. The time difference made it tricky for them to talk after he finished work, but she stayed up late on several weeknights to partake in some naughty fun over the phone.

When they'd first started discussing his visit, the original plan was for him to spend half of the trip with his friend in Queens and the other half with her. They were both cognizant of how they'd rushed into things to a certain extent and wanted to stay sensible while navigating what came next.

Until one phone call two weeks before he was due to fly out.

After a robust bout of phone sex, he spoke impulsively. "I don't want to stay with my friend."

Orgasm-brain robbed her of an articulate response. "Huh?"

"I'm crazy about you. I'm straight-up falling for you, April. And I don't want to spend any second of this trip with anyone other than you."

Her heart had kicked back up into a pitter-patter. "Nick..."

"But if it's too soon—I mean, I know this isn't the most conventional relationship—"

"You know I don't care about that," she interrupted. "It's just unconventional now. That won't last forever. Of course you can stay with me the entire time."

"Yeah?"

"Yeah." She paused and then whispered, "I'm falling for you too."

With that memory in the forefront of her mind, she

stood with him by the baggage carousel, adoring how he effortlessly draped his arm around her shoulder and pulled her tight to kiss her temple. Seeing him in person again only solidified her feelings. The distance wasn't ideal, but they'd figured out a plan that worked for them. This visit was the first step in that process.

After he retrieved his luggage, she led him toward the AirTrain. While in the station terminal, he took her hand and teased, "I could really go for a gin gimlet right now."

She glanced at him with a smile, beside herself with bliss. "You and me both."

And as a slew of New Yorkers blurred past them, they stepped onto the train and started their next chapter together.

THE LIBRARIAN AND THE MECHANIC

BLURB & CONTENT NOTES

After ending an emotionally abusive marriage, Mallory Moran has worked hard to rebuild her life in a peaceful small town upstate. Her new job at the library has helped her heal, but it hasn't alleviated her loneliness—although the handsome mechanic who frequently roams the book-stacks might.

Of course, she'd have to build up the courage to *talk* to him first.

Joel Foster is the epitome of stoic when he checks out his weekly book, but his impassive behavior keeps Mallory's secret crush at bay. Until she finds herself on the side of a remote country road with a broken-down car. Suddenly thrust into each other's orbits, the librarian and the mechanic realize they might be more on the same page than they once thought.

But when news spreads that Joel's ex-wife is back in town, Mallory is forced to confront her emotional scars and decide if she's ready for a new chapter—or if it's time to close the book on her second chance at love.

Content Notes: explicit sex, past emotionally abusive relationship (on page references), panic attack (on page), parental death (off page)

ONE

A romance novel?

Mallory Moran struggled to school her features. He normally read thrillers. Sometimes a horror novel or memoir was placed onto the circulation counter, but he'd never branched out any further than that. As a librarian, judging a patron's reading habits was the greatest faux pas, but suppressing her reaction was the ultimate challenge. To be fair, she adored a good romance novel and had even read this exact one with her book club last month. Nevertheless, the idea of *this man* reading a shamelessly steamy book made her head spin.

Perhaps he didn't realize it was a romance. The recent trend of discreet covers could be difficult to navigate if one didn't know any better.

"Your hair is lighter."

The statement hung in the air, her ears ringing as if a bomb had detonated. They'd never exchanged anything other than basic pleasantries—*How are you* and *Fine, thanks* and *Have a good day* and *Thanks, you too*—so her eyes rose to gawk at him in disbelief.

When she didn't immediately respond, his frown deepened. He tended to scowl, which should have unnerved her, but she found it oddly soothing. After falling victim to a man whose captivating smile masked devastating lies and master manipulations, she considered glowers to be far more welcome.

Mallory was staring. But, in her defense, it was easy to get caught up in every aspect of him—his strong jaw, pillowy lips, and the ink-black hair that curled at the nape of his neck when it was humid, highlighting the sprinkle of silver strands. Even his grease-stained hands enthralled her on a regular basis. Yes, she could ogle him all day if given the chance, hence why she typically lowered her head to avoid eye contact when he approached the circulation desk every Friday afternoon.

People in small towns talked, so she'd pieced together bits of information about him. Other than his general reading habits, she knew his name was Joel Foster, he owned the town's auto repair shop, and she had a dreadful crush on him.

A child's shriek interrupted the excruciating silence between them, followed by gentle motherly scolds from the nearby children's section. It was enough to shake Mallory out of her stupor.

"Yes, it is," she choked out. "A little. I got highlights."

"It looks nice," Joel said plainly. Matter of fact, even. Not a hint of flirtation to be heard. But it was enough to completely unravel her.

In the spirit of the upcoming summer season, she'd splurged on a blond balayage. No one at work had commented on the change, but she chalked it up to how the highlights naturally blended into her light-brown hair. But he'd noticed, and that only added fuel to the fire that was her silly infatuation.

It was embarrassing to harbor a crush at her age. Such things were better suited to schoolgirls loitering at their lockers, counting down the days until they'd get their braces removed. Crushes weren't for thirty-six-year-old women. But considering everything she'd endured the last few years, Mallory chose to take it as a sign that she wasn't a lost cause. That her ex-husband hadn't broken her completely.

Heat rushed to her face as she fumbled with opening the front cover of the book. After quickly scanning the barcode, she tucked the checkout receipt between the pages. But instead of her habit of placing the book on the mahogany counter and sliding it toward him, she actually handed it over. And then the moment she'd purposefully avoided for months happened.

Their fingers brushed.

Her inner swooning eighteenth-century maiden was activated, the simple touch of his skin enough to send her to an early grave. All the warmth centralized in her face shot down like a bullet train and pooled between her legs. The level of arousal was staggering enough that she quickly withdrew her hand and cradled it against her torso as if she'd been burned.

But he hadn't grasped the book fully, and it tumbled to his feet. She watched with horror as it fell, the entire sequence so distressing it was almost in slow motion. In a futile effort to stop the inevitable, she reached over the desk to catch the novel, only to knock over a container of pens and the tiered tabletop literature stand of programming flyers. Everything scattered to the ground, culminating with the booming slap of the book as it hit the original hardwood floors, the sound reverberating through the quiet library.

That was a surefire way to kill the sexual desire pumping through her veins.

"Oh my God," she bemoaned. "I'm so sorry."

He held up a hand to silence her, then bent over to retrieve the wayward items, starting with the leaflets. "It's nothing. Don't worry about it."

What a disaster. She'd spent many lonely nights dreaming about the impossible moment when they'd finally discard their routine of rudimentary small talk. How the woman she'd once been would reemerge to charm him with some witty repartee, and his frown would transform into a lustful smile, and they'd escape to the stacks for a torrid tryst.

Instead, she'd made a fool of herself.

When he rose to his full height and placed the pens back in the container, she recalled the first time she'd laid eyes on him. Since she was of small stature, everyone was tall in her eyes. In actuality, Joel was likely just shy of six feet, but he was as burly as a bull. His sheer physicality was a sharp contrast to the sereneness of the library, and one peep of him strolling through the stacks made her rush in the other direction as if the hounds of hell were at her heels.

Despite that adverse reaction and quick getaway, she'd also imagined him pushing her against the shelves to run his teeth down the length of her neck. Nothing better than good old cognitive dissonance.

Later that night, she'd ordered her trusty vibrator and soon indulged in a library-set fantasy, with him as her leading man. Facing him the following week had been difficult, but there'd been no avoiding it—he was a creature of habit and never missed a Friday visit to the library.

And the fantasies hadn't stopped there. Although, if

anything could douse her lusty daydreams completely, it would be today's spectacle.

"Thank you," she murmured, gesturing halfheartedly to clarify. "About my hair. No one else noticed."

He did a double take, his eyes narrowing. "You're kidding me."

Irritation was threaded into the timbre of his baritone voice. Mallory shook her head in silent reply, not keen on aggravating him further. The muscles in his throat strained like he wanted to say more, but all that emerged was an indignant scoff.

Eventually, he tucked the book underneath his arm, then rubbed his hands against his jeans. "Have a nice weekend."

Back to the usual script.

"You too," she muttered.

Soon he was out the door, her heart rate returned to normal, and the day continued.

But no, she wasn't a complete lost cause. Because, hours later, her fingers still sizzled with the memory of his touch.

THE PAIN of the past could barrel at someone like a monster truck, and it was usually in the most inopportune places. For Mallory, it was prompted by a particular scent. As she sat in the rustic tavern alongside her book club, the smell of her ex-husband's cologne tingled her nostrils. Her spine turned to ice, and she glanced around warily.

"You look like you've seen a ghost," said her friend and boss, Vivian.

She hadn't, thankfully. The skinny hipster who'd walked past wearing her ex's cologne looked nothing like him. Pushing down the distress, she focused on Vivian and forced a smile. "Just a bit tired."

Vivian considered her carefully before jumping back into one of the numerous conversations happening around the table. The ten women of varying ages and backgrounds were packed around a rectangular high-top table. Several wine glasses littered the space, plus two cheese and charcuterie boards that were nearly picked clean. It was Thursday night, and the bar was bustling, with soulful songs playing over the sound system.

When Mallory started as the library's circulation supervisor, the director, Vivian, took her under her wing. And after years of struggling to establish a book club with regular attendance, Vivian had dubbed Mallory a genius when she suggested meeting at a popular bar a few towns away instead of in the library's all-purpose room. *Equal parts bookish discussion and night on the town*, she'd called it, and Vivian had been wild over the idea.

The group had thrived over the past few months. Not to mention how it helped ease some of Mallory's crushing loneliness. Book club reminded her of how things used to be —when she had heaps of friends, never-ending plans, and the world at her feet.

Until *he* happened.

The club spent the first half hour discussing that month's book, but now that they'd all indulged in some libations, town gossip was the ruling topic.

"Guess who I saw walking down Main Street yesterday," Vivian said to the cluster of women, tucking a strand of brassy red hair behind her ear.

Karla, the head barista at the bakery below Mallory's apartment, perked up. "Who?"

"Christine."

"You're lying!"

"Swear to God." Vivian lifted her hand as if under oath and then snatched her wine glass, sipping the liquid with a speaking look.

"Who's Christine?" Mallory asked, glimpsing around at everyone for clues.

Despite nearly a year in town, she felt like the odd woman out during moments like these. It was one thing to be raised in a small town or move there to start a family, but it was another thing entirely to infiltrate one as a single adult.

After spending her adult life in an urban metropolis, she'd never expected to settle upstate in a town charming enough to be named Honeysuckle. It had been an adjustment—cars instead of subway trains, the whistle of wind instead of trucks hitting potholes—but she finally considered the small town her home. And the center of her world was the Honeysuckle Public Library, a picturesque Dutch Colonial stone structure on Main Street, surrounded by a garden of colorful wildflowers and honeysuckle bushes.

Inside, the stacks were cramped, and some of the amenities were outdated, but cozy nooks and crannies adorned the space. Armchairs were nestled in corners, paintings by local artists were affixed to the walls, and there was even the original stone fireplace from when the building was first constructed as a home in 1798. The entire place was the very definition of quaint. A bona fide dream come true.

And the weekly appearance of a hot mechanic was a bonus.

"You know Joel Foster?" Ariana asked, reading her mind. As the principal of Honeysuckle's sole elementary school, she found adult outings like book club essential. "He runs the auto body shop in town?"

"Oh, uh, yes. I know of him, I mean. I don't know him personally. He comes into the library sometimes, that's all," Mallory finished pitifully before gulping her semidry riesling.

The amused look on Vivian's face proved that her explanation wasn't anywhere near as smooth as she'd hoped it would be.

"Christine's his ex-wife," Karla told her. "They broke up, what, three years ago?"

Julie, the recently retired circulation supervisor whom Mallory had succeeded, grabbed a grape from the cheese board. "Maybe four."

Instead of irrational jealousy, solace settled over Mallory. Divorce was a common occurrence nowadays and didn't hold the same stigma it used to, but her status as a divorced woman produced an overwhelming sense of otherness at times. Hearing that Joel was also divorced created an uncanny comfort in her bones, as if they belonged to the same exclusive yet painful club.

Ariana raised her eyebrows. "You think she's trying to win him back?"

Vivian scoffed. "Wouldn't you if your ex looked like that?"

Laughter and titters rippled over the group, whereas acid burned in Mallory's stomach. Ah, *there* was the jealousy. She'd barely spoken to the man—last week's pitiful encounter notwithstanding—but the possibility of Joel reconciling with his ex-wife made her stomach twist like a churning sea.

But at the end of the day, crushes were irrational.

Before Mallory could subtly probe for more information, Vivian tilted her head and said, "Wait a second. Mallory, did you do something to your hair?"

Everyone turned toward her, and realization dawned. Compliments flew, and the conversation soon changed topics. An hour later, the waiter cleared the table, and chairs scraped the barroom floor as everyone stood to depart, exchanging hugs and goodbyes.

"Make sure to place your vote for next month's book by Monday morning," Vivian called out. "Stop by the circulation desk to submit your choice if you haven't already."

A chorus of replies followed, everything from *Thanks for the reminder* and *Did it already* to *Can we get some steamier options next time?*

When Mallory walked back to her car, Vivian's piece of town gossip pushed her thoughts toward a subject she'd been actively avoiding. Her therapist broached the topic of dating during their last session, but she hadn't given serious thought to getting involved with another man. Her emotions were too raw, her self-esteem still too battered.

But it went beyond simply dating again. Once upon a time, she'd been a true social butterfly, full of zest and moxie. Hell, she was even considered downright impulsive a vast majority of the time. But that devil-may-care attitude had brought her to a certain bar on a certain day and into the path of a certain man. The perfect target for a love bomb, and she'd fallen hook, line, and sinker. Heartache and trauma had followed, but she desperately missed the woman she'd once been. Oftentimes she wondered if that part of her was dead completely or buried somewhere deep inside, waiting to be resurrected.

But when it came to the topic of men, the crush on Joel had formed as a safety net of sorts. Secretly indulging in an innocent infatuation allowed her to view a man as a romantic partner again, as opposed to a manipulative monster bent on destroying her self-worth.

Granted, her vibrator would probably argue with the label of *innocent infatuation,* considering how overworked the poor toy was.

Nevertheless, continuing to construct a fantasy world around Joel wasn't healthy. And as she sat in the silence of her vehicle, keys dangling in the ignition, she had to admit that it was time to get back in the saddle and squash this ridiculous fixation once and for all.

Time to breathe life back into the woman she once was.

She grabbed her phone and downloaded a popular dating app she'd heard Karla mention before. The bio she crafted was simple enough.

Mallory Moran, 36.

Librarian. Looking for genuine connection and kindness.

After uploading a few photos to the profile, she tossed her phone into her purse, eager to ignore it until the next morning. While proud of herself for dipping her toes back in, it wasn't wise to immediately dive into the deep end.

Impulsive-ish. That'll do for now.

The engine sprang to life as she turned the key before pulling out of the parking lot, heading back toward Honeysuckle. It was after dusk, and her yellow headlights cut through the dark, illuminating her path as she steered down the long and winding country roads. It had taken several weeks to get comfortable with driving after spending much of her life relying on public transit, but she now enjoyed the freedom it provided.

What she *didn't* enjoy was how her car suddenly went haywire, the dashboard lights flashing as the vehicle jerked in an abnormal manner. Alarm surged through her as she pulled to the side of the road, wincing at the clanking sounds that roared from under the hood. Then the car stalled completely, and she rested her head against the steering wheel for a few seconds, praying under her breath.

She tried the ignition.

No dice.

"Shit. Shit, shit, shit."

Relief burst from her lungs when she grabbed her phone. One bar of service. Not much, but it was something. Dead zones were a normal occurrence upstate, and after years in the city, she still hadn't adjusted to how easy it was to be totally unplugged from the world.

Her hands trembled as she unlocked the home screen and scrolled to the maps app. It took a while to generate, her heartbeat pounding the whole time, and she shrieked with triumph when the pin finally dropped. She made a mental note of her current location, then drew the map toward the main hub of Honeysuckle.

And there it was—Foster Auto Body.

It was after normal working hours, so she had no clue whether anyone would answer, but she was desperate with a capital D. Ringing sounded in her ear as the call connected.

As luck would have it, a male voice that was *not* Joel's picked up. "Foster Auto Body, how can I help you?"

"Yes, hi. This is Mallory Moran, and—"

"Oh, sure. The librarian. How's it going?"

She hadn't expected her reputation to proceed her, but that was a thought for another day. "Uh, not great. My car's broken down, and—"

"No worries, we'll send a tow right out. Where are you?"

Remembering her pinned location on the map, she gave a general description of her whereabouts, hoping her clues were enough to locate her.

"Yeah, I know exactly where you are. Sit tight," the man instructed. "Be there soon."

The call ended, and she rested her head back against the seat. The night had taken a sharp turn downward, but help was on the way. And Joel was likely out at a romantic dinner with his ex-wife—or perhaps they'd moved on to reunion sex by now—so there was no chance she'd have to face him.

TWO

Of course Joel was behind the wheel of the tow truck that pulled in front of her car half an hour later.

"Fuck my life," she muttered, rubbing her eyes with her palms.

She lifted her gaze as he descended from the vehicle, his movements easy and assured, as if he often rescued helpless women from the side of country roads. Since it was futile to avoid the inevitable, she forced herself to open the door and step out of the car. Gravel crunched beneath her retro-inspired heeled Oxfords as she approached.

"Hi," she greeted him, raising her hand in a pathetic wave. Without the safety of the circulation desk between them, she now felt terribly exposed.

He looked her up and down, sending a shiver through her body. "You okay?"

Ah, that explained the once-over. He was concerned, not burning with attraction.

Get your head out of the clouds and back on your body, Mallory.

"I'm fine. Just embarrassed."

His brow pleated, and his ever-present frown deepened. "Nothing to be embarrassed about."

"Sorry, I—uh—I didn't realize your shop was open so late. I just took a chance and called," she admitted.

"Sometimes my cousin Tony is there past closing time. You caught him right before he left. But we have a twenty-four-hour emergency line. You would've been transferred if no one had picked up."

Still, that didn't explain why Joel came to her aid instead of the aforementioned Tony. That circumstance niggled in the recesses of her mind as she scurried over to the passenger seat and grabbed her purse. Then she stood on the side of the road as he went to work, first checking under the hood.

"Have you had trouble with it recently?" he asked, his eyes darting around as he inspected the car's body parts.

If only he'd inspect my *body parts.*

Lord, her libido was an absolute menace. She composed herself and said, "No. Although cars aren't really my bread and butter."

"Lucky for you, they're mine." After another minute of examination, he slammed the hood down. "It needs to go to the shop. I can't fix it here."

He prepared the tow and started fastening the wheel lift under her front tires. Fireflies lit up around him, a sign that summer was well and truly on its way. Joel appeared otherworldly as the glowing bursts encircled his impressive form, his biceps and back muscles undulating like some ancient Greek god. Old Mallory would've made a flirtatious little remark while admiring him—calling him Hercules or Achilles or whatever mythical hero popped into her head.

Current Mallory remained silent.

Once the front of her car was hitched to the tow, he

wiped his hands on the front of his jeans and then looked around. "You have someone coming to get you?"

The question rendered her mute, but a pitiful answer formed in her brain.

No one's coming to get me because I have no one.

She rummaged in her bag for her phone, a deliberate action to stifle the anguish eating at her dignity. "Uh, I could call Vivian—"

"No need. I can give you a lift. Just wanted to ask before offering."

The mere thought of sitting beside him made her stomach somersault like a gymnastics team, but there wasn't any guarantee she could reach Vivian or even a taxi company. Might as well endure a bit of awkwardness if it meant getting home in one piece.

"Thank you," she breathed. "I'd appreciate that."

He nodded away her gratitude and then walked to the truck's passenger side, opening the door for her.

It was, quite possibly, the most gentlemanly thing she'd ever seen.

Sure, the bar was so low it was literally in hell, but his thoughtfulness moved her tremendously. Trying to play it cool, she made the short trek over and hoisted herself into the seat. Soon after, he hopped into the driver's side, and then they were en route to Honeysuckle.

A searing silence formed, the only reprieve the radio and the sound of the wind whooshing past the open windows. But as the minutes ticked away, an unspoken serenity seeped into the air, making the moment feel simple but somehow significant at the same time.

"Nice night," Joel rumbled.

The low pitch of his voice dried her throat. Thanks to the forced proximity, she could practically feel an inherent virility pulsate from him. Her jean jacket was a small blessing, and she pulled the denim closer together, hiding how her taut nipples pressed against her knit top. Thanks to her modest 32AA cup size, those bad boys were laughably noticeable while hard.

"It is," she mumbled, peering at him from the corner of her eye. "Very nice."

His hands squeezed the steering wheel, and tension wound through his arms and upper body. When his head twisted toward her, Mallory averted her gaze and tried to concentrate on the rural roads. But as the wind whipped her hair and the radio serenaded them, she could've sworn she heard a resigned sigh from Joel.

The phone vibrating in her purse was a welcome distraction. She expected a text from her parents or perhaps a spam email but was stunned at what flashed on the home screen.

You have a like!

So much had happened in the past hour that she'd already forgotten about the silly dating app. Dumbfounded, she stuffed her phone back into her purse, but it vibrated again seconds later.

"Oh my God," she mumbled, pulling her cell out once more. Sure enough, there was another notification.

You have a message!

"You're popular, huh?" he stated, cutting through the silence.

"Um. No. Not really." She shut her phone off before it could buzz for a third time. "Just this dumb app I'm already regretting downloading."

His jaw clenched. "Ah."

The finality of that one word suggested that the conversation had ended before it'd even truly begun. But another question from him broke through the quiet.

"Where were you coming from?"

"Book club." Her voice was uncharacteristically falsetto, so she cleared her throat. She also seriously contemplated opening the door and doing an action-hero roll out of the car to put herself out of her misery. "We meet at a bar over in Kingston."

"What did you read?"

To avoid another squeaky reply, she pulled the trade paperback out of her purse instead of rattling off the title. He quickly glanced over and asked, "Did you like it?"

One shoulder lifted into an indifferent shrug. "It was okay. I think the author thought the story was much deeper than it actually was, if that makes sense?"

His mouth curled up. "It does."

As much as she appreciated his constant scowls, the little quirk of his lips was ten times more breathtaking, and she desperately wanted to behold that grin again. She could easily continue the conversation by asking about the book from last week, but discussing a story where sex was a focal point wasn't a wise idea—not when she was stuck in a car with him and shamelessly wanted to jump his bones.

Inhaling deeply, she noted the scent of cedarwood. The masculine aroma stirred her senses further, and fantasies of them tangled up in bed billowed through her brain. But before her imagination ran wild, Vivian's piece of gossip once again reared its ugly head. Mallory hadn't the faintest idea what his ex-wife looked like, but her daydreams suddenly shifted from images of herself entwined with Joel to some faceless woman. So, in lieu of continuing the conversation like a mentally balanced adult, she remained quiet.

One step forward, two steps back. It seemed to be the name of the game with her.

Just when she thought things couldn't get worse, a piece of her past intruded. The radio segued into a new tune, and familiar chords made her sick to her stomach.

The first dance.

Without thinking, she reached over and changed to another station. His eyebrows rose at her immediate reaction, his head turning a fraction to glance at her. But then he returned his attention to the road without comment.

"I'm sorry," she apologized in a hushed tone. "That was rude."

"It's fine. Not a fan of that one, I guess?"

"No." She paused, wanting to explain, but was unsure if it was appropriate. To his credit, he didn't push, and perhaps that was what compelled her to admit the truth. "That was the first dance at my wedding. I never even liked the song, but my ex insisted on it."

The air in the car turned heavy. When he didn't answer immediately, she slammed her eyes closed. Painful memories emerged like a riptide, threatening to take her under—the passive-aggressive insults, masterful gaslighting, and insidious belittlement.

And the women.

The women he had insisted were just friends, acquaintances, perfect strangers. The women he said she was crazy to worry about when, really, she'd been right all along.

"I understand," Joel eventually murmured, his words quelling the mental echoes of her past.

An undercurrent lined his delivery, suggesting that his reply wasn't an empty mollification. Maybe he really did understand. That helped Mallory regain her composure, but the sting of the song lingered, and all she could do was focus on the roadway ahead of them. They didn't speak again until the truck reached the exit leading toward the main business area of Honeysuckle.

"Where should I drop you?" he asked, putting on the blinker and smoothly making the turn.

"Black Cat Bakery is fine. I live in the apartment upstairs."

In next to no time, he pulled up outside her building. Mallory unbuckled her seat belt and finally faced him. Moonlight filtered into the truck and emphasized the faint five o'clock shadow on the slopes of his cheekbones. Compassion blossomed in his eyes, but it never morphed into pity, and that was the sole reason why she held his gaze.

The way he studied her was different—his frown wasn't as pronounced, his brow not as furrowed. He stared with quiet contemplation, as if she was a puzzle he was finally starting to piece together. And while dozens of questions bounced in his soulful brown eyes, he waited for her to take the lead.

"Thanks for the ride," she said, tugging idly at a strand of her long hair. "And for coming out so late."

"It's no problem. I'll try to take a look at your car tomorrow. We have a few customers ahead of you, but I'll do my best to get to it."

"Should I stop by and fill out some paperwork? Make a payment? I'm not really sure how this works." She laughed sheepishly and scratched her head. "I'm used to subway delays, not broken-down cars."

There was that small smile again. Butterflies flapped violently in her stomach as he shifted in his seat and pulled a business card from his back pocket. And, once again, their fingers grazed as he passed it over. At least this time she didn't pull away like she'd foolishly grabbed a hot plate.

Instead, she calmly slipped the business card into her purse and then removed her car key from her keychain.

Now it was her turn to hand something over and endure another brush of skin. But this time, he hesitated for a fraction of a second, wiping his hands once more on his jeans before he took the key. His fingers were long and broad, the nails cut to the quick. They were always streaked with grease despite his attempts to clean them, and dirt lingered beneath the nails, but they were proof of physical labor. Evidence of a man who wasn't afraid to get the job done. His hands were as captivating as the rest of him.

"We'll settle payment when the work is done. You can call the shop for an update," he said, placing her key in his pocket for safekeeping. "The number's listed there. Or I can just touch base when I see you tomorrow."

"Tomorrow?" she sputtered.

"At the library?"

Tomorrow was Friday. She'd nearly forgotten. Two Joel encounters in one week. Would wonders never cease? At least she could partake in full conversations with him now, even if they were fraught with awkwardness.

Progress. Give yourself some credit.

"Of course, tomorrow. Sounds good." She opened the door and stepped down from the truck. "Thanks again."

"Good night, Mallory."

Her name on his lips almost made her stumble off the curb. How exhilarating to know she was a real person to him—something more than just the librarian. But between that, the compliment on her hair, and how he'd rescued her from the side of the road, her feelings were dangerously close to advancing from innocent crush to full-blown obsession.

Thank God for dating apps.

"Good night, Joel." She closed the door of the truck and started toward the staircase that led to her second-story apartment.

"Hey, Mallory?"

His voice stopped her in her tracks, her stomach jumping as she turned around. The windows were still down, and he leaned over to address her, keeping his pitch low.

"No one really noticed your hair?" he asked, the question laced with incredulity.

Almost a week later, and he still looked perturbed on her behalf. It was a bit twisted to find pleasure in his irritation, but it was somehow akin to a warm hug. Isolation had been the sum of her life for far too long—first when her ex-husband masterfully separated her from her family and friends, and then when she moved upstate to start over on her own. Work and book club helped alleviate some of the disconnect, but she never felt like anyone was in her corner.

Joel's frustration that no one noticed her hair was probably the best she'd get. So she savored it, holding it close to her heart.

"People noticed tonight," she told him with a reassuring nod. "Better late than never."

His chest deflated as he released a massive breath. "Good. That's good."

Awareness teemed in her blood as she ascended the stairs to her apartment. When she placed the key in the knob, her eyes flickered down to the street. The truck idled there, waiting for her, and it didn't peel off until her door was closed and she was safely inside.

If only book club wasn't rife with town gossip. If only she'd never heard the name Christine. Because if Mallory didn't know any better, she might start to think she had a chance with him.

LUCKILY, the Honeysuckle Public Library was within walking distance from her apartment. Before heading to work, Mallory stopped at the bakery to order a coffee and pastry from Karla, and the rest of the morning passed without incident.

Except for how her phone continued to blow up with dating app notifications. She hadn't expected to get so much interest, nor did she think there'd be so many single men in her region. Because of the overwhelming response, she hadn't answered any messages yet. But she had a plan for that night—pick up some sushi, crack open the bottle of white wine chilling in her fridge, and then dive into vetting profiles and crafting replies. Surprisingly, Mallory was actually looking forward to it.

Until that time, she focused on work. The library belonged to a consortium, allowing for patrons to request books from other public libraries in the county and easily retrieve them from their local branch. The transport van stopped by that afternoon, and Mallory was sorting through the stack of requested books when Joel walked in, right on time for his regular Friday visit.

And because she was a walking disaster, the entire pile of books tumbled to the floor. Apparently, that was her new schtick when it came to him—avoid eye contact, stammer, drop books, wash, rinse, repeat. She yelped and knelt down, wishing against common sense that he hadn't noticed, but he hurried over to the circulation counter.

"You okay?" he asked.

"I'm fine," she squeaked. Then she laughed manically, because why not go for broke and *really* embarrass herself? "Clearly, I'm a terrible Jenga player."

That pitiful joke amused him if the tiny smile was any indication. He placed his book into the returns slot and waited until she got the rogue pile of novels back under control.

"We're a little slammed at the moment, but your car should be ready by tomorrow," he told her.

"Oh, good. That's great. Awesome."

One of those would have sufficed, numbnuts.

She bit her bottom lip to cease her rambling, but his eyes dipped to her mouth. And *that* didn't help douse the fire that constantly threaded through her at the mere sight of him. Unfortunately, she wasn't wearing her denim jacket today, and her nipples puckered against her emerald silk blouse. She crossed her arms over her chest, hoping his eyes wouldn't sink lower.

"We have reduced hours on Saturday. Open until three. Are you here the whole day tomorrow?" he asked.

Indeed she was, as library hours were nine to five, Monday through Saturday. "Uh, I'll see if I can come by on my lunch break..."

He shook his head easily. "Just head over whenever you can. We'll probably still be there, just not taking customers past three."

"Okay, sure. I'll do that."

Conversation over, he headed to the new-releases shelf, and his large hands perused the hardbacks, opening the front covers to skim the blurbs. He handled each one so carefully, and her mind wandered to how those same hands would handle her willing body.

As he drifted deeper into the stacks and out of sight,

Mallory refocused on the tasks at hand. Minutes passed as she sent email notifications to patrons who'd requested books, then situated the copies on the pickup shelf behind the circulation desk. Soon, a delicious shiver coasted up her spine, and she peered over her shoulder. Joel was back at the counter, ready to check out his new book.

"All set?" she chirped, attempting a level of casualness she didn't achieve. Especially once her eyes widened like a cartoon character when she saw what he'd selected.

It was the same novel she'd shown him last night—the latest book club selection. In fact, she'd put that exact copy back on the shelf that morning, having returned it herself.

"Figured I'd see for myself how deep it is," he said.

Mallory could've sworn there was a hint of huskiness in his voice, but when she caught his gaze, his face was the same as always—slight frown, intense stare, nothing out of the ordinary. So she mentally dispelled that wishful thought and scanned his library card.

"You'll have to let me know what you think," she said, tucking the receipt between the pages.

"I'll do that."

She handed the book over, as it would be asinine to continue avoiding any skin-to-skin contact. The gentle brushes of their fingers were becoming downright ordinary. Nothing to get in a tizzy about.

Yeah, tell that to your nether regions.

Joel tucked the book under his arm, and his eyes shifted downward to her cell phone sitting next to the keyboard. Another notification from the dating app lit up the home screen, and she quickly turned the phone over.

"Sorry. How unprofessional," she uttered, embarrassed beyond belief.

He didn't acknowledge her apology with anything other than his usual scowl, which seemed to have intensified. Eventually, he swallowed thickly and said, "See you tomorrow."

"Yes. Tomorrow."

Then he was out the door, giving her one last shot of his bite-worthy backside before she went back to work. The after-school crowd barreled in a few hours later, and Vivian finally emerged from the storage room she'd been working in all day. She plopped into the chair beside Mallory and sighed wearily.

"Nothing exhausts me more than the book sale," Vivian said, stretching her arms above her head.

The biannual book fair was the library's biggest fundraiser. The last sale had occurred mere weeks before Mallory joined the team, back when she'd been crafting lattes alongside Karla at the bakery. She'd taken any job available when she first moved to Honeysuckle, desperate to pay the bills. In addition to being a barista, she'd also worked as a dog nanny for the Burton family, who owned the grandest house in town.

But when Julie, the longtime circulation supervisor, decided to retire, word got to Mallory. She had prayed for months that she'd somehow wiggle onto the library staff, and the stars aligned perfectly. Considering her past experience as associate director of adult programs at the city library's main branch, she was a shoo-in for the job—was honestly overqualified when it came down to it.

And yet, there was a bone-deep need to prove she was an invaluable asset to Vivian. Mallory's life revolved around this building, and it was imperative to do whatever she could to hold on to it.

"I had an idea, actually," Mallory began.

Vivian's eyes sparkled. "You know how I love your ideas."

"What do you think about organizing a silent auction? I can solicit donations from local businesses. Gift cards, things like that. Could be a good way to boost funds."

"Brilliant, as always. Run with it. Let me know if you need any help shaking down storefronts," Vivian added with a grin. "And you know what I realized? Next Saturday is also your six-month anniversary."

Mallory glanced at the desk calendar. "Oh, wow. You're right."

"We have to do a formal evaluation. Let's plan for the following Monday since the sale will keep us busy."

She gulped at the words *formal evaluation.* Like many jobs, the library had a six-month probationary period. Yet another reason why she'd gone above and beyond—coming in early, leaving late, and spearheading programming efforts. Anything to show that she deserved to stay. Deserved to belong.

"Sounds good," Mallory replied with a restless nod.

Vivian noticed her unease and gave her a supportive smile. "Just a formality. Nothing to worry about. Hell, you'll be running this place in my stead one day."

The assurance alleviated some of her nerves, but not all. Her time in Honeysuckle had provided a smidgen of stability, but a large piece of her still felt terribly unmoored. As if everything she'd worked so hard to establish could disappear in a single instant. The rug had been ripped out from under her once before, and now she lived with that possibility forever in the back of her mind.

Maybe she'd finally feel some semblance of security once her probationary period was in the rearview mirror. Maybe she could relearn to trust people after her sense of self was razed to the ground. Maybe the old Mallory she yearned for could be revived.

Maybe, maybe, maybe.

When she returned home later that evening, she toed off her flats and donned her house slippers. Sushi was ordered and wine was poured, and she opened the windows to let the evening breeze into the ordinary one-bedroom apartment. After dinner arrived, she settled on the couch and waded through the app messages.

There were a few creeps, a few with questionable politics, and one whose features reminded her way too much of her father. But two profiles held promise, so she sent basic replies to both. The entire process was draining, but a sense of accomplishment bubbled within her once she finished.

More progress.

But through it all, she tried not to think about cruising down the country roads with Joel at her side.

THREE

Foster Auto Body stood at the tail end of Honeysuckle's business district, right before Main Street went from shop-lined to rural. A large plot of land sat next to the slate-gray building, with several cars clustered on top of the gravel, Mallory's included. The garage doors were closed, and the place appeared locked up tight as she approached.

It was after five in the evening, and although Joel had instructed her to arrive whenever, she should've called to confirm someone was still there. But a small light illuminated the office window, and she breathed a sigh of relief once she peeked inside. Because Joel sat at one of the desks, his feet propped up and a book in his lap.

Encouragement bloomed in her chest, her silly crush now at DEFCON 1. The shop closed hours ago, yet here he was, waiting on her arrival. But pesky rationality pulled her back down to earth. The man ran a business, and she owed him money, so he'd stuck around to collect. Nothing more, nothing less. She tapped on the window to get his attention, and he coasted a few steps over to answer the door.

"Hi." She did that pathetic little wave once again. "Sorry I'm so late."

"Nothing to apologize for. I told you to come by whenever."

As per usual, he looked good enough to eat. He stepped back to allow her enough space to enter the compact room, and she did her best to appraise him without calling attention to herself. Dark jeans hugged his muscular thighs and mouthwatering ass, and his upper body was encased in a threadbare T-shirt with a faded Foster Auto Body logo across the chest. The hem of the shirt was frayed and smudged with years' worth of grime, but he wore it well.

It would also look fantastic chucked away onto the floor. Alongside his pants, of course. But that was neither here nor there.

Somehow, she tore her eyes away from him to inspect the office. There were two desks, both adorned with time-worn computers, and the one Joel had sat behind was particularly tidy—files and paperwork stacked nicely—whereas the other desk was a war zone of unruly items. Black filing cabinets lined one wall, and wedged beside them was a mini fridge with a microwave stacked atop it. An ancient coffee maker rested on a filing cabinet, rounding out the feeble attempt at a kitchenette. A large corkboard rested on another wall, covered with different memories—photos and old holiday cards and an adorable drawing depicting *Uncle Joel and his wrench*, the words written in shaky, childlike penmanship.

Joel grabbed a few pieces of paper from his desk, then placed them back down just as quickly. His throat bobbed as he reached over to a pile of rags sitting atop a filing cabinet and used one to wipe his hands with haste. Then he returned to the papers.

"Pretty standard stuff," he began, then proceeded to explain her car's diagnosis and the work he'd performed. It was all mumbo jumbo to Mallory, but it was evident this man was an expert in his trade.

Competence porn galore.

Despite her attempt to hide her reaction when reviewing the bill, she didn't succeed. He noted her expression and said, "If you need to set up a payment plan—"

"No, no," she interrupted, rummaging in her purse for her credit card. "It's okay. I've got it."

Since joining the library full-time, she still often worked shifts at the bakery on her day off to supplement her income. This unexpected expense meant she'd definitely spend the next few Sundays preparing cappuccinos and plating pastries.

Joel ran her credit card, and she signed the receipt. With payment settled, he returned her car key and handed over the statement of work for her records. The conversation was due to dwindle down, but it seemed like a prime time to build on the personal progress she'd made so far. No need to let her silly crush get in the way of acting like a mature adult.

"What do you think so far?" she asked, pointing to the book on his desk.

"I agree with what you said." Picking it up, he tilted his head in thought before thumbing at the pages. "Not all that deep, but it's trying to be."

Ah, to have someone validate her opinions instead of tearing them down. So simple yet unfamiliar to her. It made her ravenous to continue talking to him. "What about, um... the book from last week?"

A smile spread across his face, showing off a dazzling set of white teeth. Mostly straight, but a few were a tad cramped, as if he'd had braces as a child but lost his retainer and never replaced it. "What about it?"

There was a coy tinge to the question, and her knees knocked together. "Did you like it?"

"It was different. But yeah, I liked it."

Time for the question she'd dwelled on for days. "Did you realize it was a romance?"

"Figured as much. The blurb hinted at it."

Ah, the blurb. Mallory nodded vigorously as if she'd already come to that obvious conclusion herself. Another question danced on her tongue, but he beat her to the punch.

"I saw you reading it a few weeks ago," he said, tossing the current book back onto his desk.

The confession stunned her. "Huh?"

"One Sunday at the bakery. I was walking by to grab lunch. You were totally engrossed in it, so I figured I'd give it a try."

"Oh," she mumbled, the word so hushed she almost didn't hear herself.

After months of paltry interactions at the circulation desk, she'd assumed that her new hair color was the first time he'd ever truly noticed her. But here was proof that that wasn't the truth.

Something suspiciously like hope tingled in her heart, and the sensation was so unfamiliar she didn't know what to make of it.

He leaned onto the edge of the desk and crossed one ankle over the other, his powerful thighs straining against the dark denim. "What made you want to become a librarian?"

The answer was simple, so she shrugged. "I like books. What made you want to become a mechanic?"

"I like cars."

Delight stampeded throughout every inch of her. Not only was it adorable that he'd followed her lead, but it hit her like a ton of bricks that they were flirting.

Flirting!

Goddamn, but it was fun to flirt. Back in the day, it had been her favorite pastime. Her city friends used to joke that she'd flirt with anything with a pulse. All innocent fun, although the frivolity had turned fraught soon after her wedding.

But in the here and now, the dopamine rush was irresistible—her blood pumped, and stress whittled away, and conquering the world seemed feasible. She smiled so broadly that her cheeks hurt, no different from a smitten schoolgirl in homeroom.

His jaw sagged in response, but he hastily snapped it shut. The intensity permeating from his whiskey-colored eyes became so overwhelming that Mallory's gaze eventually lowered to the floor, as it often did while in his presence.

A weighted silence stewed until, finally, she gestured to the door. "Um, I don't want to keep you..."

"You're not keeping me from anything."

Nevertheless, a stalemate was incoming. She shifted on her feet, keys jangling in her hands, and snuck a peek up at him. His brows knit together as he looked into the distance, collecting his thoughts.

"That's not true, actually. I haven't always liked cars," he admitted wistfully. "I became a mechanic because I wanted to master them."

"What do you mean?"

"My parents were killed in a car accident when I was a kid. I thought if I learned everything about cars, I'd make sure nothing like that ever happened again." A tiny chuckle escaped him as he crossed his sculpted arms across his chest. "The dreams of a child, clearly. But when I got older, I realized I was good at it and could make a career of it. So here I am."

"I'm so sorry about your parents. I had no idea."

A somber smile flickered over his face. "Why would you?"

Indeed, why would she know such a thing? It wasn't like they were friends. They were barely even acquaintances. Regardless, she focused on the photos on the corkboard, keen to learn everything about him. A faded polaroid of an attractive couple and a boy with unruly ink-black hair caught her attention. The boy smiled so fiercely that his eyes were closed, and his two front teeth were missing.

"Is that them?" she asked.

Joel grinned, happy memories shining on his face. "Yeah. That was my seventh birthday. Batman themed, naturally."

"Naturally," she agreed, returning his soft smile with her own.

"The crash was about a month after," he recounted, rising all the way to his feet. "Then I came here to live with my aunt and uncle and cousin Tony."

He'd arrived in Honeysuckle after experiencing a trauma, same as her. Granted, they were wildly different circumstances, but it was still meaningful to Mallory—just as they shared divorced status, this small town had been a form of salvation for them both.

"Didn't mean to turn this into a therapy session." He shook his head and placed his hands on his hips. "Sorry about that."

"Oh, no! Don't apologize. I don't mind at all. I love hearing this sort of thing."

Her face burned like a furnace once the words left her mouth. Good God, what was the matter with her? She attempted to recover, sputtering out incoherent placations.

"Not—I mean—oh my God. I don't mean that I *love* hearing that your parents are dead. That's not what I mean at all. I would never say something like that. I know I sort of said it, but I didn't *mean* it. I just—I was trying to say that—"

His steady voice broke through her unhinged apology. "Mallory. Take a deep breath, okay?"

Her hands were clammy, sweat trickled from her brow, and her chest was a stone's throw away from collapsing. She was no stranger to panic attacks, but it had been a while since she'd last experienced one. The response was visceral enough to feel like the first time—when she had attended her ex-husband's company's holiday party soon after their wedding, had a tad too much to drink, and acted a bit too cheeky for his liking.

The ride home in the taxicab was the first time in her life she'd been referred to as a *fucking worthless bitch*. But it hadn't been the last time, and it wasn't the only cruel insult she'd heard that evening. And later that night, she'd locked herself in the bathroom and endured the panic attack alone, certain her heart would explode.

"I know that's not what you meant," Joel said, bringing her back to the present. He took one hesitant step forward like she was a skittish animal. "It's okay. Just keep taking deep breaths."

She obeyed, closing her eyes as she shakily pulled air into her lungs. Unfounded thoughts delivered in her ex-husband's voice swirled through her.

There'll be no facing Joel again after this.

He'll tell everyone how damaged you are.

You should quit your job and move out of Honeysuckle.

You'll never belong anywhere again.

Each sentiment was more out of control than the next, and although part of her knew none of it was true, that sensibility was held hostage by the strength of her anxiety.

When he gently took her hand, her mind shifted. He tapped the pad of his callused finger against her palm over and over, and her consciousness latched on to that steady action. The continual pressure against the softness of her skin had a soothing effect, and soon her heart rate began to stabilize.

"Breathe. Good. That's it. There you go," he reassured her, keeping their hands linked. "Does that happen a lot?"

"Sometimes." The confession was quiet as her eyes fluttered open. "But it's been a while. Not since..."

Not since she'd moved to Honeysuckle. Further proof that she'd made the right decision to restart her life in this charming little town.

"Do you want to sit? I can get you water, or—"

She shook her head as assertively as she could manage. "No. I should...I should go."

"I know it's not far, but if you need me to drive you home, I can—"

A shrill ring broke into their hushed conversation, making her jump. She glanced over at the cell phone sitting on his desk and laid eyes on the caller ID.

Christine.

The name was a gut punch, knocking the wind out of her. More memories undulated her already fragile thoughts—the secretary, the waitress at the pub around the corner, their wedding planner, the bottle girl during the bachelor party, the friend from college, this woman, and that woman, and every woman.

It had been so easy to forget about Joel's reunion-seeking ex-wife, thanks to all their eventful moments over the past few days—including how incredibly thoughtful he'd just been. But when it came down to it, she couldn't allow these lingering feelings to cloud the progress she'd made the last few days. She'd be doing herself a disservice if she continued to get tripped up by him.

So she pulled away from his supportive grip, her arm dropping to her side. "No, it's okay. I can drive."

He silenced the call, sending it to voicemail. "If you're sure?"

A weary nod was her reply as she turned the knob and stepped out of the office. "I'm sure. Thank you, Joel."

The faint words of "You're welcome" reached her ears as the door floated shut.

FOUR

Instead of spending Sunday obsessively reliving her panic attack, Mallory worked a shift at the bakery and turned to the dating app in her spare time. She'd hit it off with a guy named Tyler, a teacher thirty minutes away from Honeysuckle, and they'd already progressed from messaging on the app to exchanging texts. The conversations were pleasant enough, but it was difficult to gauge chemistry through the phone, so plans were made to meet for drinks that Saturday night.

Saturday promised to be a busy day since it was also the library's used-book sale. Considering Mallory only had a few days to scrounge up silent auction donations, she hit the ground running. Beginning Monday afternoon, she spent her lunch breaks bouncing from business to business in Honeysuckle and the surrounding towns, shamelessly soliciting contributions. Her landlord supplied a one-hundred-dollar gift card to Black Cat Bakery. The pizza joint offered a free slice per month for the next calendar year. And the yoga studio donated a complimentary enrollment in their six-week beginner workshop. Each business owner was eager to help, which boosted her confidence every time she walked into another storefront. It was the perfect exercise to continue pushing herself outside her comfort zone.

It wasn't until Wednesday afternoon that she faltered. Because once she reached the end of Main Street and laid eyes on Foster Auto Body, flashbacks from that weekend thrashed at her. She'd been dreading his Friday library visit, well aware there was no avoiding him. But seeing Joel a few days earlier would be akin to ripping a Band-Aid off, and her therapist constantly emphasized the need to conquer her tendency to cope via avoidance. Better to face the music now instead of stew in anticipation—that's what the old Mallory would do, at least. With an encouraging breath, she headed toward his establishment.

The building bustled with activity as she approached. All three garage doors were open, and the sounds of power tools and men shouting commands fluttered over the warm breeze. A burgundy SUV was hoisted in a car lift, with two mechanics working on the undercarriage, while a rusty sedan waited nearby for a new set of tires. The strong smell of motor oil permeated the air, intertwined with the aroma of sweaty men working in the early summer heat. The entire scene was intimidating, and she'd be better suited heading to the main office door, but Mallory wandered closer.

Even with all the commotion, Mallory only had eyes for Joel. He stood near the built-in shelving units lining the wall on the far side of the garage, clad in navy-blue coveralls. The top half of the garment was tied around his sturdy waist, exposing the gray undershirt that clung to his upper body. He hoisted a tire onto his shoulder, and she sweltered at such masculine strength. Her hungry eyes trailed his muscles, engrossed in how they contracted and released with exertion.

Their eyes connected the instant he turned, affixing over the hustle and bustle of the garage. His dark eyebrows rose in surprise, which she acknowledged with an apologetic smile and her quintessential small wave. He placed the tire down, leaning it against the side of the sedan. Small patches of sweat had seeped into his undershirt, and a thin sheen of perspiration covered his brow. Work gloves adorned his hands, so he used his forearm to wipe away the moisture as he drew nearer.

"Everything okay with your car?" he asked in greeting.

"Oh, yes. It's fine. Perfect, even. Runs like a dream."

One day she'd figure out how to reply to him with a straight answer, but apparently, that day was not today. She took a second to regroup.

"I'm here on library business," she told him.

"Oh?"

She quickly explained the silent auction endeavor and asked, "Would you be interested in donating something? It can be anything, really. Free oil change or something like that."

His alluring mouth twitched. "Did you suggest an oil change because it's the only thing you know about car maintenance?"

"Guilty," she joked, holding up her hands in surrender.

A soft laugh bubbled from his chest. "Put us down for a free tune-up."

Mallory nodded despite not having the slightest inkling what constituted a tune-up. She made a note in her phone, adding the item to her donation list. "Thanks. We appreciate it."

"Are you accepting books?"

"We are. The sale is on Saturday, so we're collecting until the day before. Just so long as they aren't musty and gross," she added with a grin.

Joel returned her smile with a tentative one of his own. "I'll bring some on Friday, then."

Before she could respond, a lean man with a riot of curly dark hair emerged from the undercarriage of the lifted car. Mallory was instantly reminded of her surroundings and realized the men working nearby had stopped to watch them converse like they were goldfish in a bowl.

"It's the librarian," the man stage-whispered to Joel, nudging him in the ribs. Then he turned his attention to Mallory, removing his work gloves and shoving them in his back pocket. "How's it going?"

"Fine, thanks." Recognizing his voice, she asked, "It's Tony, right?"

Tony raised his eyebrows and threw a shit-eating grin Joel's way. "She knows my name."

"Congratulations," Joel replied dryly, giving his cousin the side-eye. "You want something?"

Tony ignored the question and threw an arm over Joel's shoulder. "My cousin is a great guy, you know."

There was a joke happening that she wasn't privy to since Joel turned his head and threw Tony a thoroughly exasperated look. But, inexplicably, the silent communication made the hope she'd locked away this past weekend reemerge, knocking on her heart like a weary traveler.

She nodded in agreement and murmured, "I know."

"Glad we're all on the same page," Tony replied as he patted Joel's sculpted chest with his free hand, which Joel swatted away. The interaction brought a smile to her face; she could easily picture them as young boys roughhousing around Honeysuckle.

Joel shrugged his cousin's arm off. "Tony, do me a favor and shut the fuck up."

He said it so succinctly that Mallory giggled. An absurdly girlish sound, so she tucked her chin down against her collarbone, waiting for the unbearable embarrassment to commence. But Joel's reaction to her laughter—how victory flashed in his eyes and his already noticeable chest puffed out—kept her irrational thoughts confined.

Tony released a barking laugh and signaled to the other mechanic nearby. "We're going to lunch, boss."

"Music to my ears," Joel grumbled.

The men strolled off and headed down Main Street, undoubtedly bound for the deli or pizza joint. After witnessing the auto shop's earlier commotion, the stillness was significant as she and Joel stood alone. She suppressed the desire to squirm, knowing she couldn't ignore what had happened at this very location a few days prior, but the words still got caught in her throat.

He removed his work gloves and tossed them onto the hood of the sedan. As he cleaned his hands with a rag, he peered at her cautiously. "Everything okay otherwise?"

"Yes. Great. Really good, even." There she went again, a nice, plentiful bunch of word vomit. She collected herself and said, "I want to apologize for the other day—"

"Don't."

"But I—"

He looked her dead in the eye, equal parts fierce and gentle. "Mallory. I think you apologize too much." Then he cleared his throat and raised his hands in a diplomatic fashion. "Uh, respectfully, that is."

The amendment was endearing, and the negative tension in her body faded bit by bit. "I guess I was conditioned to always apologize."

"By the ex with shit taste in music?"

Typically, any reference to her ex-husband conjured a wide range of emotions. Mirth was never one of them, but Joel's forthright question made her chuckle.

"Shit person with shit taste in music," she agreed with a wry smile. "You know, he once berated me for hanging toilet paper the wrong way."

"Ah. Under?"

"Yes," she confirmed, a semblance of shame persisting.

He shrugged. "I like under. It looks aggressive when it's hanging over."

After months of fantasizing about Joel, of imagining him bending her over the circulation desk and having his way with her, she never expected an innocent comment about toilet paper would make her heart soar. But it did.

Her throat tightened, overcome with emotion. She couldn't form a proper reply or maintain eye contact. Instead, her gaze drifted lower and lingered on his chest, captivated by the small puffs of silver-tinged black hair that peeked out from the top of his gray undershirt. For a few seconds, her entire world revolved around the curve of his pectoral muscles, the vastness of his shoulders, the slopes of his biceps, and the pronounced veins in his forearms—all culminating in those large hands that handled books so delicately.

Gawking at him was nothing new, but she'd graduated to straight-up leering like an animal in heat. She dragged her attention away from his torso, eyes darting around the garage in an attempt to act natural. Even though there was nothing natural about the way she'd just blatantly eye-fucked him.

The old Mallory would be proud, though.

"I should get back to work," she muttered.

One glance up at Joel, and she abandoned that plan. A light shade of pink tinged his sharp cheekbones, and his dilated golden-brown eyes made her quiver. While no stranger to his intense looks, something was layered into his expression—something so primal her knees weakened. Because the way Joel peered at her was not the stare of acquaintances or newfound friends.

In fact, it was the look he wore in every fantasy she'd constructed since first laying eyes on him. The look that drove her to press the button on her vibrator, upping the pressure until her hips bucked off the bed. She blinked a few times, assuming she'd hallucinated the whole thing, but the sensual episode only deepened the longer they stared at each other. His stormy gaze carefully traveled down the length of her, fixating on the pebbled peaks that obscenely pressed against the linen bodice of her sundress.

Christine.

Christine.

Christine.

There was no phone call to break the moment this time —no shrill sound to pull Mallory back down to earth—so she chanted the name in her mind like the most painful incantation.

"Relationships are tough," Joel eventually rasped out, fracturing the heady silence.

"I agree." She paused and looked down at her Oxfords, so polished against the scuffed concrete floor of the garage. "Sometimes I wonder if they're worth it at all."

"They are."

His response was filled with such conviction that she lifted her gaze and caught his eyes. Every moment they'd shared over the past week rushed back to her, and her head spun with the substantial memories she'd created with him in such a short span of time.

That little spark of hope within her simply couldn't be extinguished. Not while one question remained unasked. Her mouth opened, the inquiry on the tip of her tongue.

This might be too forward, but can I ask what the situation is with your ex-wife?

In the end, she couldn't summon the courage to ask. The woman she'd once been—the one she wanted more than anything to bolster back to life—was still woefully dormant.

With a quick glance at her wristwatch, she smiled contritely. "I really do need to get back."

"Of course, yeah. I'll see you Friday."

She whirled around and proceeded down the driveway, but his rumbling voice stopped her.

"Hey, Mallory?"

"Hmm?" she said, glancing over her shoulder.

Joel stepped forward, leaning against the garage-door frame. He gestured toward her and said, "That's a pretty dress, by the way. Brings out your eyes."

The cornflower-blue sundress was nothing special, but his compliment made it feel like the finest haute couture. A smile extended across her face, and bliss zipped down from her head to her toes.

"Thank you."

The flicker in her chest billowed into a tiny fire, warming her insides, and the thawing process commenced. While not completely defrosted, she'd taken steps that had stoked the fire, and the return of the old Mallory didn't seem quite so impossible anymore.

As she walked back toward the library, there was an extra pep in her step and a goal in her mind.

Friday. She'd ask him about Christine on Friday.

Maybe there was hope for her yet.

FIVE

As fate would have it, the sky cracked open on Friday morning, and unrelenting rain poured onto the streets of Honeysuckle. Mallory continually checked the local weather radar, hoping the deluge would cease. But the forecast projected rain throughout the weekend, effectively ruining the library's plan to host the book sale and silent auction outside amid the wildflowers.

Since they hadn't advertised a rain date, the staff decided to hold the event inside the building. With many factors to rework and modify, Mallory was so preoccupied on Friday that she didn't immediately note Joel's absence. He always visited during the one o'clock hour, which came and went with no sign of him.

Suddenly, her stomach grumbled, the sound loud enough to steal her attention, and she realized she'd also skipped lunch. She grabbed her umbrella and headed to her car, thoughts swirling about Joel's whereabouts. He wasn't one to deviate from his normal routine, so she prayed everything was okay as she made the short drive over to Black Cat Bakery to order their famous French onion soup.

After pulling into the closest parking spot, she jumped out of the car and hurried to take cover under the bakery's awning, but her hand froze when she clutched the doorknob.

Through the foggy glass, Mallory saw them clear as day —Joel and a woman. A rather beautiful woman, at that. Auburn hair was pulled into a ponytail, and she wore skinny jeans with a white button-down shirt, the motorcycle boots on her feet giving her the right amount of edge. An easy intimacy lingered between them. They sat close together at a circular table, partaking in what was obviously a meaningful conversation.

Christine.

Mallory's appetite vanished immediately.

Over the past two days, she had foolishly spent hours alone in her apartment, literally practicing how to broach the topic of Christine. She'd stood in front of her mirror and rehearsed her lines like she was the starring role's understudy. When, in fact, the leading lady was right in front of her.

Stupid, stupid, stupid.

Well, what was another disappointment in the grand scheme of things? She knew better than to get her hopes up —knew better than to believe anything would come from a stupid infatuation. And she certainly knew better than to think she could ever recapture who she'd used to be. Swallowing down the pain, she returned to her car and peeled off to the library, determined to lose herself in work for the rest of the day.

But as she entered the building, her phone buzzed in the back pocket of her burgundy corduroy miniskirt.

Looking forward to meeting you tomorrow.
7 p.m. at the tavern still work?

Tyler's text was exactly what she needed. Her future was not with Joel. To be fair, it probably wasn't with Tyler either, but his message hammered home why she'd downloaded the dating app in the first place.

It was time to move on. From her ex-husband, from the painful memories of her past, from the life she once thought she'd have. There was no point in ignoring reality or living in fantasy worlds of her own making. She'd had a rough few years, but she wasn't the first woman to be broken by a man, and she was certainly not the first woman to develop a silly crush. So she typed out a reply.

7 p.m. is perfect. Can't wait!

She stepped behind the circulation desk and tucked her purse into one of the drawers. Vivian had covered the counter while Mallory grabbed lunch, and she noticed her surly mood immediately.

"What's wrong?" she asked, never one to beat around the bush.

Mallory grimaced and said, "Just upset about the rain, that's all."

Vivian gave her one of those looks—the look of a friend who knows when you're lying but also knows better than to push. She switched topics instead, handing Mallory a piece of paper.

"Here's the evaluation form for Monday. We both fill one out," Vivian explained. "Mine has the usual stuff—employee productivity, work quality, blah, blah, blah. Yours is more about goals and that sort of thing."

Mallory placed the form down before her hands started shaking. Admittedly, everything about the document was nonthreatening. Four basic questions, with small spaces beneath for each answer. But getting served with this paper after witnessing the scene at the bakery was like a one-two punch.

"Sounds good," she said, forcing a smile for Vivian's benefit.

After closing hours, the staff handled the finishing touches for the next day. Tables scrounged up from storage were placed around the edges of the multipurpose room. Popular fiction titles were arranged to make the best use of the space, with several boxes of books tucked beneath the tables for replenishing. Non-fiction went outside the all-purpose room, catty-corner the circulation desk, and the silent auction items were arranged on two tables near the main entranceway. Since that component was her initiative, Mallory dutifully spruced up the gift cards and baskets, placing each item alongside its designated bidding list.

Soon enough, everyone headed home for the night, and she offered to lock up. With the lights low, she sat alone at the circulation desk with a pen in her hand. The ballpoint hovered over the evaluation form but never touched the paper, her entire form as still as a statue.

What do you hope to accomplish as a full-time member of the library?

The first question was straightforward, yet she couldn't formulate an answer. Moving to the second question, her mind was still blank, rendered completely useless by a simple document.

A loud knock nearly sent her through the roof with fright, and her head jerked up before her gaze landed on the front door.

Joel stood on the other side, hunched under an umbrella with a book bag draped over his strapping shoulder.

When his eyes met hers and that undeniable electric current raced through her, Mallory almost forgot what she'd seen earlier that day. Almost forgot how determined she'd been after receiving Tyler's text message.

Almost.

She grabbed the keys and unlocked the door, ushering him out of the rain and into the refuge of the library.

"Sorry," Joel said, closing the umbrella and placing it in the ceramic stand near the door. "I know you're closed, but I saw your car in the parking lot and thought I'd take a chance."

"Take a chance?"

He held out the book bag. "That you were still accepting book donations?"

"Oh. Sure," she muttered.

Limply, she took the bag and headed into the all-purpose room. All his books were thrillers or mysteries, so she dumped them in the correct area and then stepped outside the room.

He examined the silent auction items and said, "You've got some good stuff here."

Back to small talk.

Nevertheless, she nodded and held out the empty bag. "Thanks again for donating. Both for the auction and the books."

"You're welcome." He slung the bag over his shoulder and grasped the lone book tucked beneath his arm. "Mind if I return this?"

"Sure."

A strangely comforting request. She shuffled behind the circulation desk, eager to return to their proper positioning.

Every time she'd been outside of this environment with him, her common sense had misbehaved like an unruly toddler. This was where they belonged. Her on one side of the counter, him on the other. Some pleasantries here and there. No more, no less.

Rain pounded on the rooftop as she checked the title back into the system. Joel waited patiently—for what, she wasn't certain—although he shifted back and forth on his feet in an antsy manner. When he wiped his hands against his jeans like he often did, a dull throb echoed in her chest in response to the odd habit.

Once she finished checking the book back in, she held it close to her chest and offered him a shaky smile. "Well, hopefully, you can swing by tomorrow and bid on an item. If there's anything you're interested in."

He cleared his throat. "Yeah, I...uh, the Black Cat Bakery gift card looks appealing."

Easier to shower Christine with coffee and pastries, no doubt. The disillusionment was so acute it was almost a physical burden on her back, making her slouch until her eyes met the ground. "See you tomorrow, then."

She moved around the counter, her Oxfords clacking against the hardwood floor. Continuing past the dormant stone fireplace, she roamed through the maze of stacks until she found the proper shelf and returned the novel to its home.

Alone among the books, she regained her composure. Seconds passed into a full minute, and then another, until she was certain Joel had departed. But instead of returning to the desk, she stood within the stacks, taking solace in this building. Sure, she might not have it all together, but she'd done something right—she'd found this place. No matter what happened, she'd always have the Honeysuckle Public Library.

So long as she aced the evaluation on Monday.

Before she could return to the desk to revisit the form, her phone buzzed in her back pocket.

You have a like!

She swiped to take a cursory glance at the profile but could barely believe her eyes.

Joel Foster, 39.

The rest of the profile was blank, and it contained only one picture—a photo of him working under the hood of a truck, his face concealed. But there was no mistaking his identity. Not when she'd memorized the shape of his taut biceps and back muscles.

"Fucking finally."

Her head lurched up to find Joel at the far end of the stack. With an irritated sigh, he shoved his phone into his back pocket and mumbled to himself, "Took long enough. Now I can finally delete this dumb thing."

She blinked rapidly, positive she'd experienced a super potent delusion. But there he stood, and his profile remained on her phone, though the planet shifted beneath her.

"I'm confused," she whispered.

That beautiful frown of his magnified. "About what?"

"Um..." She paused, unsure how to answer such a loaded question coherently. "Everything?"

He blew out a breath, adorably peeved. "I saw the app on your phone last week. Downloaded it, hoping it would match us, but it took longer than I thought. Didn't realize there were so many people on this stupid thing."

A boulder lodged in her throat, making it nearly impossible to speak. Nor could she think straight, as evidenced by how she strode toward him, grabbed his shirt, and yanked his mouth down to hers like a woman possessed.

No, not like a woman possessed. Like the old Mallory.

Hello, you. Long time no see.

Oh, but how she had missed kissing. The act made her heart flutter like a flock of doves. Made her feel desirable and wanted and like she belonged. And this kiss was explosive—an awe-inspiring fireworks display that lit up every nerve within her.

He tossed the bag over to the side, grasped her slim hips, and growled like an animal setting sight on its prey. Before she knew it, her body was pressed against the shelves, his burly physique crowding her. Lush lips that tasted as sweet as powdered sugar coaxed her mouth open without protest, and the skillful stroke of his tongue riled up her insides. She rose onto her tiptoes and threw her arms over his shoulders, digging her fingertips into the firm muscles. The feel of his body was indescribable. Lightyears beyond the fantasies that had fueled many a masturbation session.

They broke the kiss to gulp in air, and the fact that she'd mauled him with no warning plagued her. "I don't know what came over me. I'm so—"

Mighty hands cupped her face, tilting her head back. "Don't you dare apologize," he commanded. "Not now, and not with me."

There wasn't time to form a rebuttal, because his mouth descended and obliterated the unreasonable contrition. The lust she'd attempted to control completely unleashed, her good reason was nowhere to be found, and all that remained was the incredible sensation of his lips against her own. A tiny part of her knew this path led to disaster, but she couldn't bring herself to care. Tonight was the time to let her old self run free, to bask in spontaneity, and to finally indulge in the ultimate fantasy. Consequences were inevitable, but she'd face them tomorrow.

Her hands burrowed under his T-shirt, trailing the ridges of his abdominal muscles. Joel hissed in pleasure, his head lolling back as her exploration continued to the downy hair across his pectorals. His chest lifted with a trembling breath, and then he ground his erection against her pelvis without a hint of shame. The act was so blatantly sexual that she whimpered hoarsely, clamping her thighs together to try and generate a bit of relief.

But it was no use. What she needed was his fingers. Those gorgeous hands.

"My skirt," she whispered.

"Up?"

With a hasty nod, she urged, "Yeah."

"Thank fuck."

In a flash, he pushed the fabric up around her waist, revealing her white cotton panties. They groaned in tandem when he cupped her mound, and her head slumped against the books behind her as he rained kisses along the side of her neck. She widened her stance to provide easier access, marveling at how deftly he stroked the damp fabric. When he pushed the cotton to the side and trailed his index and middle fingers through her soaked folds, she cried out.

"Ah, fuck." His free hand groped her tiny breasts, tweaking the rigid buds through her button-down blouse. "Do that again."

"Do what?" she panted.

His fingers found her clit and rubbed in circles, drawing a ragged moan from her mouth. A satisfied smile brightened his face. "That. God, *that* sound."

And when he pushed one long finger inside her, she sobbed. Her head sagged, resting against his bicep as she struggled to pull air in and out of her lungs. The unrelenting pumps created a delicious tension, and her inner muscles fluttered when his thumb lavished attention on her clit. He added a second finger, stretching her even further, and she feared her legs would give out as she trembled at the knees. Her hands frantically grasped at his sturdy frame, desperate to hold on to anything solid.

"Don't let me fall," she stammered.

Even with such a lust-addled brain, she knew there was much more to that plea.

Don't let me fall for you.

"You're okay. I've got you," he assured her.

His free hand cradled her face, moving her head to drink her in. Despite her earlier brazenness, she immediately shut her eyes, the vulnerability too much to bear.

"Don't do that," he begged in a reedy voice. "You never look at me. Fuck. *Please.*"

The earnestness in that plea granted her the strength to obey. When their gazes met, her heart kicked into overdrive at the undiluted hunger etched into his features—like he wanted to fuck her until she could barely breathe, then softly kiss every sadness away.

His fingers curled, reaching her G-spot, and her body jolted at the powerful sensation. Her climax was within reach and promised to be frighteningly potent. She gyrated her hips to gain momentum, and he groaned unabashedly.

"That's it," he grunted. "Ride my hand. Ah, fuck, you're driving me fucking crazy."

Immersed in a cloud of lust, she reached forward and squeezed the impressive bulge straining against his jeans. The deep growl he emitted washed over her like warm honey. But when she fumbled with his belt buckle, his free hand captured her wrist.

"You first," he ordered, pinning her arm back against the shelf. "We have all night."

"Joel—oh my God—" she gasped as tremors overtook her. "Oh God, oh God."

The orgasm took root low in her belly, surging into a peak of powerful pleasure. A ragged scream ripped from her throat as her body quaked, her pussy clamping around his talented fingers. Although she tried to keep her eyes on him, they rolled into the back of her head as she surrendered to the euphoria.

His arm wrapped around her waist, keeping her upright as her body wilted, riding out the final twitches. But she never worried about crumbling completely. He had her, just as he'd promised.

A mischievous voice tickled her ear as his fingers retreated from her core. "I thought librarians were supposed to be quiet."

Even though she was spent, a hearty laugh tumbled from her. It was exactly the type of joke the old Mallory would've quipped, and it boosted her spirits further. She swept her fingers through his dark hair, admiring the softness of the strands, and used the leverage to guide his lips back to hers.

God, he was perfect. *This* was perfect. She never wanted it to end; she wanted to savor every last bit of him.

"Do you have a condom?" she whispered against his glorious mouth.

"I think so. Fuck, I hope so."

"Find it."

As he reached into his back pocket, she dropped to her knees. Her shaky hands undid his belt buckle, going through the motions until his cock sprang free, jutting out from a thatch of black hair. No surprise—his shaft was thick like the rest of him. Not overly long, but so meaty, her hand barely wrapped around it.

He groaned when she grabbed the thickness, the sound awash with lust. Almost comically, he waved a foil packet near her head, which she took absently, letting it fall to the floor beside her. They'd take advantage of the condom later. Right now she wanted to make use of her mouth.

Leaning in, she wrapped her lips around the column of hard flesh and sucked deep. Remembering his earlier words, she kept her eyes on him, mindful to maintain the connection.

"Oh, *fuck*," he boomed, chest hitching.

Always the epitome of strong and steady, Joel's slow unraveling was immensely satisfying to watch. How he babbled profanities, and one arm tensed as he clutched the shelf, and his other hand lifted his T-shirt enough to give her free rein. She stroked his cock with one hand, moving in time with her mouth, coating the rigid skin with her saliva.

"Oh my *fucking* God," he growled in a tone no different from gravel. "You're gonna kill me. That feels so fucking good."

Releasing him from her mouth with a pop, she gulped in air. "Take it off. Your shirt."

Joel heeded her order, lifting the fabric over his head. She thought it impossible to get wetter after such a mind-blowing orgasm, but another gush of arousal materialized at the sight of his bare chest. Her eyes wandered over the landscape of beautiful brawn before she returned to tending to his cock.

A sound rumbled from him—something between a groan and a laugh—as he idly played with her hair. "This is the hottest thing I've ever seen in my life."

The admiration poured off him, bathing her with confidence, and she looked up with ardent eyes. Desperate to please him, she took his cock deep, holding it at the back of her throat for as long as possible. His eyes widened, the light grip around her hair tightened, and otherworldly noises thundered from him.

"The condom," he heaved once she withdrew for air. "Put it on."

The packet was ripped, and the condom rolled down the length of him. Joel pulled her to her feet, her knees tender after kneeling against the hardwood floor. Shaky legs somehow held her upright as her panties were swiftly removed, exposing her lower body completely. His trembling hands tried to unbutton her blouse but couldn't manage quickly enough. The buttons popped off as he ripped the fabric apart, scattering to the ground like the raindrops outside.

"I'll get you another one," he promised.

"I don't care."

His response was guttural. "I care, Mallory."

The words were the worst kind of taunt, but she ignored any fanciful notions of a deeper meaning. Ignorance was easy to maintain when he pulled her bra down and uncovered her breasts.

"Fuck. So pretty." He slanted down to suckle both nipples and then issued a command. "Arms around my shoulders."

Once she complied, he hauled her up like she weighed no more than a feather. Being surrounded by such potent strength made her gasp, and she trembled when he arranged their bodies properly, notching his rigid shaft against her pussy. Her mind spun at the standing position. Not only had it been ages since she'd last had sex, but she hadn't indulged in anything other than the three reliable scenarios of missionary, cowgirl, or doggy style in such a long time.

"Open up and sink down onto me. That's it," he praised when her inner muscles relaxed and succumbed to the size of his cock. "Oh, fuck yeah, that's it."

Both were mostly clothed—his pants around his thighs, and her skirt up and blouse hanging loosely—but it elevated the torridness of the entire encounter. Wedged against the bookshelf with her legs wrapped around his waist, Mallory relished the erotic feel of their bodies joining. It took a few seconds to adjust to the powerful invasion, groans and gasps sounding from both as she reached the hilt.

"Okay?" he asked in a hush.

A rapid nod was all she could manage. Their pelvises connected, and his massive hands squeezed her backside, barely restrained lust written in the action. His whole body pulsated with the urge to take her.

"Fuck me," she pleaded in a needy tone. "Please."

"Yeah?"

"Please, please. I need it."

"Yeah, you do," he growled, satisfaction interwoven into the words as his hips retreated and then thrust forward. "You gonna look at me while I fuck you?"

"Yes." When he withdrew and buried himself deep again, she cried out, the sound hoarse. "Oh God, yes. Whatever you want."

That reply spurred him on, his movements picking up speed. She made an effort to move with him, but the positioning had her entirely at his mercy. All she could do was hold on tight as he pinned her against the books and fucked her senseless. His face contorted in pleasure, and his incredible frame vibrated with exertion as he pounded her. Every thrust was urgent, as if he had something to prove.

The sound of their bodies created a lewd soundtrack, the sexual slaps mixing with the steady thumping of the rain outside. Her moans escalated, and a second climax coiled within her as he continued his relentless pumping. The entire situation was so beautifully obscene that she could barely breathe.

As if reading her thoughts, he leaned in for an open-mouthed kiss, granting her his breath. "You want to come again, don't you?" he whispered against her lips. "I can feel it."

Words failed her, so she nodded and dug her fingernails into the skin of his shoulders.

"Don't hold back on me, okay?" he said, the rhythm of his hips becoming erratic.

"I won't. Oh God, Joel. Oh, oh, oh—"

For a second time, her pleasure crested, all the nerves in her body detonating with mind-blowing sensation. It was the first time she'd orgasmed without direct clitoral stimulation, and the pulses, while not as intense, were slow and steady and earth-shattering—just like Joel himself.

"This is fucking unreal," he rasped. "Fuck, Mallory. Oh, fuck, I'm gonna come."

The shelf dug into her shoulder blades as he nailed her with chaotic thrusts, his body spasming with heightened passion. He kissed her as he came, the act severe and tender and perfect. His lower body jerked as he emptied himself into the condom, and Mallory clung to him desperately, knowing that, soon, reality would infiltrate.

Joel held her in his arms as they both recovered, their dueling gasps slowly fading into the rainfall. Time passed, although it was not nearly enough for her.

"I'm gonna put you down," he warned her.

She wanted to protest, but instead, she whispered, "Okay."

Carefully, he brought her legs to the floor, and she was no different from a recently born foal learning to stand upright. Her hands remained on his broad shoulders, using his burly body as a support system until she was steady on her feet.

As he handled the condom, shuffling over to toss it into a nearby wastebasket, thunder cracked for the first time all day, an indication that the storm was worsening. And that sharp crash pulled Mallory out of her sexually infused state.

Gone was the woman who'd been celibate for ages and needed someone to strum at her body like a world-class orchestra. Gone was the woman who regularly cried in her apartment, the insurmountable loneliness a crushing weight on her shoulders. Gone was the woman who downloaded a dating app, hoping she might be able to trust a man again.

All that remained was the librarian. A librarian nearly at the end of her probationary period, at that. And when she saw the mess she'd made—the books that had fallen from the shelves, the puddle of her arousal seeping into the hardwood floor—panic engulfed her. For God's sake, she hadn't even locked the door behind Joel. Anyone could've entered the building and seen them rutting like a pair of animals.

She had nothing to show for herself other than this library. It was the most important relationship in her life, and she'd endangered it. All for a man who'd been canoodling with his ex-wife mere hours ago.

This is what you get for reviving the old you.

Hysteria and shame joined forces, bringing every possible worst-case scenario to the forefront of her mind. And that was why, when he returned and leaned in for a kiss, her hands shot to his chest without thinking.

She pushed him away and said, "You need to go."

SIX

"You want me to go?" he asked, the question low and hoarse.

His stricken features almost made her weep, but dozens of feelings battled for dominance. Because no, a huge part of her didn't want him to go. Especially not when he looked so devastatingly handsome—all rugged and wild after their frantic coupling. His torso glistened with perspiration, and the dark strands of hair were tousled. Her ultimate fantasy now a reality.

But profound dread was winning the emotional war raging within her.

She hastily pulled her skirt down, setting herself to rights—at least as much as she could when her blouse no longer contained any buttons. Her eyesight floated to the mess on the floor, and the disarray sent another tremor of terror through her. Heavy breaths sawed in and out of her lungs as she knelt and grabbed her discarded panties, then used the fabric to wipe away the droplets of moisture on the hardwood.

"Yes, I want—I want—you should just—" she stammered, her brain so scrambled that lucid sentences were a chore.

Joel knelt beside her. "Mallory, it's okay. Just talk to me."

"I can't, I can't. Oh God."

One large hand tenderly clasped her own. "Deep breaths."

"This is *not* a panic attack," she snapped, pulling away.

Her ferocious reaction momentarily stunned her, even though she'd spoken the truth. Panic attacks were extreme reactions to threats that were often not based in reality, but the danger she'd created was alarmingly tangible. She was overcome with the magnitude of what she'd done. Of how she'd threatened her livelihood and betrayed his relationship with Christine all in one night.

"Then what is it?" he asked, a measure of bitterness embedded in his tone as he grabbed his T-shirt and wiped his hands with it.

"It was a mistake."

The lie burned her mouth. Made her want to shriek with anguish. But she said it nonetheless, and his entire form jolted at the insult. Her refusal to look at him was only making the situation worse, but she'd crumble completely if she lifted her gaze to his own.

"A mistake," he repeated slowly, his delivery devastating.

"This shouldn't have happened." To her horror, the tears she'd tried to subdue broke free and streamed down her cheeks. "Please. Just go."

Joel's labored breaths rippled with distress, but he didn't respond. With her head lowered, she felt him rise to his feet, heard him buckle his belt, and then the heavy steps of his work boots pounded the floor as he departed. The slam of the front door pulled a sob from deep within her, the sounds of her grief mixing into the cacophony of the storm.

The rain didn't stop, nor did her tears. They trickled down her face as she gathered the fallen books and placed them back onto the shelves, a librarian to the very end.

AS EXPECTED, the rainfall continued, and it didn't help Mallory's wretched mood. But she went through the motions, arriving at the library early to prep the volunteers working the book sale. Traffic was slow when the doors opened at nine that morning, but it picked up an hour later and remained steady. People went wild over the silent auction, the bids climbing as the day went on.

Mallory wished she could enjoy it, but her spirits were muddied by last night's events, and guilt ate away at her as each hour passed. The blank evaluation form taunted her from the desk, and she could barely fathom getting through her date with Tyler that night. Especially considering how her whole body ached, deliciously sore after last night's exertion.

She wasn't surprised one iota when Joel didn't make an appearance at the sale. The gift card for Black Cat Bakery was destined to belong to someone else, and something as trivial as that made her heart ache alongside her body.

When closing time rolled around, Mallory and Vivian sat behind the circulation desk and counted the profits while the rest of the staff and volunteers packed the leftover books, stashing them away in the storage room until the next sale. Once the winning bids for the auction items were factored in, Vivian's hands raised with elation.

"That's double what we made in the last sale," she whooped.

Mallory managed a tight smile. She collected the last few dollars and placed the cash in the lockbox. "I'll email the winning bidders on Monday."

"We'll have to make the auction a new tradition. Fantastic idea, Mallory."

The praise fell flat, and shame threatened to swallow her whole. It hadn't even been a full day since she'd hooked up with Joel, making a mess of this place, and she could barely look Vivian in the eye. How was she supposed to keep this secret and continue working here? It might mean losing her job—losing everything she'd worked so hard to establish for herself—but she couldn't function if she didn't come clean.

"You know Joel Foster?" Mallory began, her stomach in knots.

"Rawr. Sure do."

A pitiful laugh flew out of her, and she hid her face in her hands. "He stopped by late last night to drop off some books. We may have, um...kissed," she confessed, simplifying the situation to lessen the blow at first.

"Oh, good for you," Vivian said, patting her thigh lovingly.

Mallory lifted her head to gawk at her boss. "Huh?"

"I knew you had a little crush on him. Glad one of you finally made a move."

Vivian's casual reaction wasn't what she'd expected, but when Mallory considered it further, it wasn't all that surprising. Her boss was the epitome of chill, and she was her friend to boot. Granted, Vivian's opinion might alter if she heard things had progressed beyond a kiss.

"I feel terrible. It really wasn't appropriate to let him in after hours…" She trailed off, still unable to admit to the full truth.

"Mallory, he could've bent you over this desk and banged your brains out and I'd still be happy for you."

Well, then. Guess that settles that.

All that worrying for nothing. Served her right. But the knowledge that her position at the library was secure despite last night's transgressions only raised her morale slightly.

She leaned back in the chair, sighing with defeat. "Even still. It's not like it'll work out."

"Says who?"

Mallory threw her a look. "Christine, obviously."

"Uh, you definitely don't have to worry about that."

Confusion swirled like a whirlpool. "What do you mean? At book club, everyone joked that she was trying to win him back."

"Key word there being *joked*. I don't know why she's in town, but trust me. If she did want to rekindle things, Joel would not be on board."

"Why not?"

Vivian struggled with how to answer. "God, where to even begin? I don't know everything, and what I do know is hearsay. But it was bad. And I love to gossip as much as anyone, but you should ask him yourself."

Exactly what Mallory originally planned to do before witnessing yesterday's interlude at the bakery. Angst churned in her belly, the possibility that she'd jumped to conclusions a tough pill to swallow. She'd been so programmed to believe things would never go her way that it was effortless to default to the worst-case scenario. While she wasn't positive exactly why Joel met with Christine yesterday, she'd never know the truth if she didn't ask.

Evidently, all that introspection was written over her face, because Vivian gave her shoulder an encouraging squeeze before she lifted the lockbox and tucked it against her shapely hip. "Don't you have a date tonight?" she asked.

Shit. Mallory glanced at her watch. She was due to meet Tyler in an hour. She'd suggested the book club's favorite tavern as the location for their date since it was a reliable spot. But it meant she'd have to depart soon to arrive in time, especially if the roads were rougher than usual, thanks to the rainfall.

"Yeah, I do," she admitted resignedly.

"Hmm."

She snorted at Vivian's astute answer, and her boss winked before heading back to her office. As the rest of the volunteers finished for the day, Mallory touched up her makeup. Even though there was an urgency to learn the truth from Joel careening through her like a rushing river, she was at a loss when it came to the next steps.

The sensible course of action was to follow through with tonight's date and resolve things with Joel at a time when she wasn't teeming with one emotion after the other. Her return to impulsive behavior had already contributed to one meltdown this week, so it was best to play it safe.

Haven't you played it safe enough?

Mallory shoved away that internal remark before it got the better of her. Before heading out, she folded the evaluation form and slipped it into her purse. She'd take care of it in the morning, confident she'd be prepared come Monday.

But as she neared the door, she almost tripped over her feet when she noticed that the ceramic stand contained one umbrella—Joel's. She hadn't realized he'd left it last night, and irresistible memories surfaced, threatening her resolve.

I care, Mallory.

Nevertheless, she forced herself to continue with her plan, although she grabbed the umbrella before leaving the library. The rain had eased off, now more of a mist than a deluge, and she set off on the usual route toward the tavern. As she traveled the familiar roads, the windshield wipers moving every minute to sweep away the light drizzle, a familiar sensation wormed its way into her chest.

Flashbacks of that fateful ride home with Joel consumed her. How the wind had coasted through her hair, and the moonlight had danced over the planes of his forearms while he clutched the steering wheel. How the energy between them had vibrated and coiled, so palpable that she'd been an utter fool to believe it was all in her head.

Sometimes the simplest things—a ride home here, a compliment there—could shift your entire world. And as she approached the exact location where her car had broken down, it was evident that another significant moment was destined to transpire. This time she'd have the courage to embrace it fully.

Because her earlier thought was right on the money. She'd played it safe for too long. Last night's events notwithstanding, of course. She swerved to the side of the road and parked her car. The roads were quiet, but she put her flashers on as a precaution and grabbed her cell phone. As expected, the dating app took a while to generate, thanks to the spotty service.

When she pulled up her matches page, her heart plummeted to the ground. Joel's profile was gone. He must have deleted it completely. There went her brilliant idea to message him. To use it as a tool to put herself out there and clear the air between them.

Go big or go home, Mallory.

She scrolled through her call log and found the number

for Foster Auto Body. With bated breath, she waited for the call to connect.

"Hello, you've reached Foster Auto Body. We're sorry we can't come to the phone right now. Please press one to leave a message, and we'll get back to you as soon as we can. If you need emergency assistance, please press two."

This might not constitute an emergency in the grand scheme of things, but nothing felt more important to Mallory. She pressed the correct button, still unsure what she'd say if Joel picked up instead of his cousin. Thankfully, Tony's voice reached her ear.

"Foster Auto Body," he said. Faint noise echoed in the background, almost as if he'd stepped away from a gathering.

"Hi, Tony. It's Mallory."

"Ah, the librarian. Hello again."

His tone was playful as usual, and she suspected Joel hadn't told him about last night's events. It strengthened her resolve to follow through on her impulsive plan.

"My car's broken down," she lied.

"You've got shit luck, huh?"

"You have no idea. But I'm hoping that changes soon."

He laughed and asked, "Where you at?"

"Same exact spot as last time."

There was a slight pause, and she could almost hear the wheels turning in his head. "What a coincidence."

"It is. Any chance you can send the tow out?"

"I'm in the middle of something right now...but pretty sure I can get my cousin to take care of it," he quipped, catching on straightaway.

"Don't tell him it's me, okay?"

"Why not?"

The memory of Joel's distraught face hardened her throat. "I'm afraid he won't come if he knows."

"Lovers' tiff?"

"Something like that," she conceded.

"I'll tell him it's a helpless old biddy, how's that?"

Close enough, she thought wryly. "Perfect. Thank you."

With the plan in motion, she sent a message to Tyler, apologizing profusely for canceling their date at the last minute. He replied back almost immediately, showing a gracious level of understanding, and suggested rescheduling for the following weekend. But there was no point in pursuing things further. Not when her sights were set on only one man. After respectfully declining Tyler's offer, she deactivated her account on the dating app.

The minutes passed as she waited on the side of the road, her heart and hope on the line.

SEVEN

Headlights broke through the haze as the tow truck approached a half hour later. Like last time, it parked in front of her vehicle but idled for several seconds. Joel didn't emerge, suggesting he'd recognized her car and put two and two together.

Time to be brave, Mallory. You owe it to him. Even more importantly, you owe it to yourself.

Full of determination for the first time in years, she opened the door and stepped out. The sprinkle of mist was so minor that she didn't bother with his umbrella. In truth, the rain's cleansing sensation only bolstered her faith as she marched toward the driver's side of the truck.

Joel stared straight ahead, his hands still clutching the steering wheel. His brow tightened when she neared the window, implying he saw her in his periphery, but he closed his eyes to take a fortifying breath. Alarm weaved into his expression when he finally glanced over.

The door shot open, and he descended from the truck. "For Christ's sake, don't stand around in the rain."

A soft smile swept over her face. "I kind of like it."

Clouds darkened the sky above, but the never-ending storm inside her soul was clearing, a shimmer of sunlight befalling her for the first time in ages. The work was only beginning, and it would be a long and arduous process, but fear no longer imprisoned her.

"You can wait in the truck until I finish." He moved past her, bound for the tow. "I don't want you getting sick."

"I've been sick for ages. But I think I'm finally starting to get better."

It was pointless to hold on to the woman she'd once been, no reason to yearn for a triumphant return. The old Mallory was a mere memory at this point, and it was okay to finally let her rest. What mattered now was moving forward and how she used her past experiences to guide her toward a positive future. Toward a happy and healthy, brand-new her.

"And I don't need a tow," she said, fessing up to the scheme.

Joel stopped and placed one hand on the edge of the truck bed. The tables had turned, as now he couldn't look at her. His stare remained on the rain-soaked gravel, and his throat worked with unsaid sentiments.

"I'm sorry I freaked out," she whispered.

"You didn't just freak out. You *cried*."

She winced, the consequences of her tears beginning to take root. He rubbed his hands against his jeans, and she instinctively reached out to thread their fingers together.

"You always do that," she murmured, brushing her thumb against his skin.

A puff of defeated laughter left his lush lips. "Nervous habit."

"I...I make you nervous?" she asked, bemused.

He returned that puzzlement with a raised eyebrow.

"Mallory. You're a librarian. You literally wore a tweed jacket once."

"What's wrong with my tweed jacket?"

"Fucking hell, nothing's wrong with it. Made me hard as a goddamn rock, if you must know." He massaged the bridge of his nose with two fingers, mortified in the most endearing way. "What I mean is...listen, you're from the city. You wear tweed and corduroy and those shoes with the laces and the heels. You spent months ignoring me. Wouldn't look me in the eye."

Those words gripped her lungs, squeezing the air out of her as his point of view came into hyperfocus.

"Shit, I even saw you numerous times at the bakery. Tried to catch your eye when you worked there, but nothing," he continued.

Mallory racked her brain, unable to recall any memory of Joel before the time she saw him in the library stacks and rushed in the other direction. But she rarely worked the register at the bakery, always delegated to the barista counter, and, on top of that, the fog of anguish she inhabited during that time had her unable to think straight most days.

"Then you started working at the library, and you literally ran away from me." He laughed, the sound despondent, and his massive shoulders lifted into a shrug. "What the hell was I supposed to think?"

"Oh God," she lamented, partaking in a true-blue facepalm. "That's not at all—shit. When you put it like that, I sound like such a snob."

"Figured someone like you wasn't interested in a guy who spends his days covered in grease. And that Friday when I checked out a book, and you pulled away from me so fast..." He trailed off, swallowing thickly as he glanced down. "I started wiping my hands, and I never stopped."

Understanding shredded her insides, and she wanted to scream at how foolish they'd both been. But, in actuality, it was a blessing they'd danced around each other for the past few months. Mallory hadn't been ready for him then, but she was now.

As such, she placed a soft kiss against his knuckles, silently communicating that his big, beautiful, callused hands were always fit to touch her. When his gaze lifted to meet hers, a stunning level of vulnerability shimmered in his eyes. Unsure how to give words to the swarm of emotions within her, she cradled their clasped hands against her heart. Droplets of rain trailed down his chiseled face as she held his stare and refused to let go.

"If you only knew how much I wanted these hands on me," she eventually confessed.

His expression shifted from dejected to cautious. "Yeah?"

"I had a huge crush on you. That's why I couldn't look you in the eye. Or do anything other than stammer. *You* made *me* nervous. And with everything that happened with my ex, I was still too...fragile, I guess."

"I started putting the pieces together after our car ride. But my pride and insecurity and all that shit held strong. That's why I downloaded that stupid app on a whim. I wanted to show I was interested, but I didn't want to push or anything—"

"I might need to be pushed sometimes. Otherwise, I'll stand still for the rest of my life."

"Even so. Not if it makes you cry."

She shook her head, praying for eloquence as she launched into an overdue explanation. "My probationary period at the library ends on Monday. I panicked that someone would find out what we did. Wild sex in the workplace isn't exactly appropriate."

He considered that, his chest rising as if inhaling her words and the weight behind them. "Fair enough."

"And I also freaked out because of the Christine factor."

Bewilderment flickered on his face. "What does Christine have to do with this? How do you even know about her?"

"Joel, you know how small towns are," she said with a shrug. "People talk. And I saw you with her yesterday at the bakery."

"Ah, hell. I didn't realize. Listen, Christine and I are not getting back together."

Hearing it straight from Joel himself was comforting, but she wanted to clarify her hasty reaction. "My ex cheated on me," she divulged. "Constantly. I lost count of how many times. And all my suspicions were turned on me, manipulated to make me think I was being unreasonable. Acting crazy. And when I saw you with her, I just..."

"I'm telling you. Christine is a nonfactor. She had a massive gambling problem. It was..." His jaw clenched, and he shook his head as if to dispel the memories. "I don't want to get into the details, but it was bad, okay? Almost-lost-the-auto-shop kind of bad. She's been in a program, and she came back to—"

"Make amends," Mallory finished for him, the puzzle finally solved.

"That's right. I was avoiding her, trying to dodge her calls, but she was persistent. And I finally agreed to meet her."

Sure enough, Mallory hadn't only jumped to conclusions. She'd full-on leaped to them like a long jump Olympian. How easy to do so, instead of believing in what they'd been building toward. It was effortless to default to the worst possible outcome, and it took all the strength in the world to have faith. But rebuilding faith—in yourself, in others, in the world—was the ultimate challenge, and she evidently still had a long way to go. But there was no place else she'd rather do the work than in Honeysuckle, with her beautiful library and maybe even with this man beside her.

"Probably should've had some of these conversations before we slept together," she joked, and his laugh warmed her insides like a hot toddy.

"Probably," he agreed with a droll smile.

"It's just hard sometimes to even *have* conversations when everything I said was twisted and—I mean, not with you, but with—"

The gentle brush of his hand against her cheek silenced her. "I understand."

"But I'm in the therapy, and I'm really trying to get better," she finished, finally rife with confidence.

He nodded, his unwavering belief in her apparent with that simple motion. As much as she craved his kiss, she desired something else even more. She flattened her body against his solid chest without pretense, and he wrapped his strong arms around her, enveloping her in a healing hug. The damp fabric of his shirt seeped against her cheek, but it didn't blot out the inferno of hope within her.

"Do you want to give this a go?" she whispered.

"I've wanted that since the second I laid eyes on you."

Her head fell back to beam at him. Joel returned the joy, his once stoic stare now radiant, and he bent down to claim her mouth in a gentle kiss that built in intensity.

"I still can't believe we fucked in the library," she said with a giggle when they finally came up for air.

His booming laugh was laden with exuberance. "I

know. Especially since I jerk off to that fantasy all the damn time."

"Same here," she confessed, loving how easy it was to chuckle with him in the rain. "I thought about it so much I almost broke my vibrator."

He wiggled his brows and said, "What about fucking in a tow truck?"

In tandem, both sets of eyes fluttered to the front seat. Without another word, they dashed off, scurrying around to the passenger side. Joel opened the door for her, ever the gentleman, although he followed that politeness with an ungentlemanly kiss, his hands gripping her hips greedily. Her skin was slick with rain, but her whole body burned for more of his touch.

Before they climbed into the truck, he blanched. A large tool bag sat on the passenger seat alongside strips of loose fabric and other garments—likely a collection of rags and spare T-shirts for particularly messy workdays. He hurriedly tossed everything away, hurling items onto the dashboard, the floor, and the driver's seat.

"It's a mess," he said with a regretful shake of his head. "Didn't think I'd—"

Mallory pushed his shoulders, guiding him back onto the seat before he finished the unnecessary apology. With a saucy smile, she climbed into his lap and slammed the door shut.

"Make a mess of me," she purred, tugging his earlobe between her teeth.

A carnal growl rumbled from his chest, and he shifted to retrieve a condom from his wallet. Placing the packet in the cup holder for safekeeping, he ensnared her mouth, and she rocked against his groin. Frantic kisses followed, each one filled with a silent promise. Pledges to communicate better, to give this their all, to not let fear get the better of them. Every brush of his lips strengthened her belief in an optimistic future.

As full as her heart was, her panties were just as damp. He gripped her ass as she squirmed against his erection, both working together to increase the friction. No different from a couple of horny teenagers desperate for some privacy. She lifted her hips when she reached her limit on the foreplay, allowing him enough room to unzip his jeans and sheath his hard cock with the condom. Her pleated midi skirt worked to their advantage, and she moved the lace to the side of her lower lips instead of discarding her underwear completely. Desire soared as she positioned herself, sinking onto his cock with a whimper.

Outside, the rain picked up again and drummed against the truck, matching her own steady rhythm as she rode him. She gathered her skirt's fabric in one arm, and Joel helped her move, completely in tune with her needs. Every inch of him was perfect, from the rigid erection to his rapt gaze. Despite the public setting, not a single car appeared on the remote road, and they only had eyes for each other.

After last night's frantic fucking, they took it slow and savored the feel of each other. Kisses, tender touches, words of affirmation. Her climax built steadily, bubbling within her like a hot spring. His thumb worked her clit masterfully until she finally burst, a cascade of pleasure sweeping over her.

Joel held her close while she reveled in the sensations, peppering her neck with heartfelt kisses. Her cadence faltered, so he took the reins and thrust into her pliant core until he reached his own orgasm with her name on his lips.

"One day we'll do it in a bed. Clothes off and all," she joked, resting her head on his solid shoulder.

"I'm not worried," he whispered into her damp tresses before pressing a gentle kiss to her temple. "We have all the time in the world."

WHEN THE BOOK sale returned six months later, the amount of silent auction donations had tripled. Since it was the dead of winter, the event was once again held inside the library, and the layout was rearranged to allow for the extra tables. A blanket of snow covered the ground outside, but inside was warm and toasty as residents from Honeysuckle and the surrounding towns came out in full force to purchase well-loved books and place their bids on the auction items.

So much had changed in six months, but the library remained a constant source of comfort. After all the anxiety, she'd aced her evaluation with Vivian days after she and Joel had stood in the rain and started their journey together. Mallory had filled out the form while lounging on his couch the following afternoon, her legs draped over his lap as he read. And during the meeting that Monday, Vivian had confided her intention to retire in five years' time, deeming Mallory as her planned successor.

But until that time, she spent her days behind the circulation counter, loving every minute of it.

Throughout the day, her eyes often drifted over to Joel. He'd broached the idea of volunteering for the sale earlier that week, insistent that Tony could handle the shop on his own for a Saturday, and was assigned a payment table. It was utterly adorable how he sat sentry over the lockbox, diligently counting out change for each used book destined to go to a new home.

He caught her gazing, their eyes locking across the library. *Love you*, he mouthed.

Love you too, she replied back.

Later that night, once staff and volunteers had tidied everything, Mallory offered to lock up. And because Joel drove them both to the library that morning, he stayed behind too.

She spent most nights at his charming cottage, located about fifteen minutes from the main hub of town and situated near a bristling brook. The lease on her apartment was up next month, and they'd recently had a frank conversation about their next steps. Although Mallory barely lived at her apartment nowadays, her prior experience of rushing into a relationship still lingered. She'd decided to re-sign for another year, simply to give herself some peace of mind, and Joel had been completely on board, happy to support her in whatever way she needed.

But that was the type of man he was, and she loved him all the more for it.

Once the lights were shut off, Mallory stopped him from putting on his winter jacket without a word. Joel sent her a questioning look, but that confusion shifted to lust when she turned the key to lock them in. She crooked a finger, silently luring him back into the stacks.

After all, it was healthy to be impulsive every now and then.

THE MAESTRO AND THE ROOFER

BLURB & CONTENT NOTES

Once a star in the music world, Mia Pelletier's fall from grace was legendary. Now the composer famously known as Maestro Mia has escaped to a coastal cottage, but her plan to create brilliant music that reclaims her legacy is derailed by a debilitating creative roadblock.

However, a storm that damages the cottage's roof produces an unexpected muse...

Travis Flynn is bold and brash, but Mia finds herself inexplicably drawn to the man tasked with repairing the wreckage. As their attraction grows, she discovers another side of the rough-hewn flirt, and soon, the famous maestro and small-town roofer learn they're actually in perfect harmony.

But as their convenient fling grows into something deeper, Mia must face the music—either return home to restore her glory or strike a new note with an unlikely love.

Content Notes: explicit sex, loss of a grandparent (off page), strained familial relationships (minor references)

ONE

Her marriage and career had collapsed, so it was fitting that the roof collapsed too.

"Hell of a storm," the foreman lamented with a shake of his head as his fellow crew member hauled a ladder out of the truck that proudly boasted *Robinson & Sons Roofing* across the doors.

The last few years of my life have been a storm, buddy. This is nothing new.

Mia Pelletier had been in the coastal town of Daymont, Connecticut, for only a few days when the tempest tore through—the worst the northeast had seen in over a decade. All things considered, she was lucky the roof was the sole problem, as several hundred people in the area were without power.

"You Leslie?" the foreman asked. He was short and stocky, with fiery red hair and a face of freckles to match. A local through and through.

"No, she's a friend," Mia replied. "She's letting me stay here for a few weeks."

Despite the decent-sized hole in the roof, the coastal

cottage was a stunning piece of property, and Leslie had offered it as a much-needed refuge. The home was classic Connecticut—creamy-white siding with sage-blue trimmings, a wraparound porch overlooking a tidal river connected to the Long Island Sound, and a rickety dock leading to the water. Inside, the home was summer themed all year long, splashed with different hues of blues and greens, and marine artwork decorating the walls.

The ultimate setting to breathe new life back into herself. But as each day passed, Mia knew the fresh air wouldn't solve her problems.

"Okay, yeah. The work order says to call her with updates," the man murmured as he consulted the crumpled paper he pulled from his back pocket. He nodded to the other crew member. "I'm Eric, the foreman, and that's Jerry. In case you have any questions. We'll stay out of your hair as much as possible."

"I'm Mia." She searched their faces for any recognition, but her tense shoulders relaxed when they didn't pay her a second glance. Then again, neither man appeared to be the target audience of Maestro Mia.

Funny how that nickname had once been a source of pride. Now it felt like a curse.

"We'll have to check out the interior damage, though, if you don't mind?" Eric said, gesturing to the door. A gentle awareness was layered into his tone—an understanding that a lone woman around two strange men could feel uneasy.

Instead of cracking a joke that she'd seen a porno that started this same way, Mia let them pass through the door, and she returned to the kitchen to brew a pot of coffee. After devouring some cottage cheese and berries, she brought a mug of steaming caffeine onto the porch. The water had mostly calmed, the waves crashing mildly against the dock's weathered pillars. It was only the beginning of October, but the air was crisp with the promise of winter.

As she curled up on the porch furniture, her ears pricked at the roar of an engine. A sleek forest-green truck barreled down the remote road, dirt and gravel flying into the air. The truck took a sharp turn and proceeded up her driveway, parking behind the roofing crew's vehicle. Then the door opened and a man stepped out, and the hair on the back of her neck stood up.

Mia had sampled a handful of men since her divorce, but none exuded the pure animal magnetism of this one. Tall and lean, he moved with swagger—just enough to prove he was a force to be reckoned with, but not so excessive to be labeled arrogant. Unruly dark-blond hair topped his head, coupled with several days' worth of stubble across his undeniably chiseled jaw.

Noticing her blatant inspection, he met her scrutiny with a charged look. Every inch of her skin burned as his striking sapphire-blue eyes examined her, moving from head to toe, the perusal eventually settling on her lips. Work boots hit the porch steps, ascending in a slow and steady manner as he approached like a predatory jungle cat.

"You the tenant?" he asked in greeting.

His voice—low and smoky and masculine—sent a bolt of heat zipping through her, but she steeled her reaction and said, "Temporary tenant. My friend owns the house. I'm visiting for the month."

"Ah."

No other comment was offered. Only a smoldering stare, which he performed well, as much as she hated to admit it. Instinctively, she pulled her chunky sweater closer, silently cursing her lack of appropriate clothing. She was clad in ratty leggings and a cardigan she lovingly called her granny sweater because it had belonged to her late grandmother. Not an ounce of makeup adorned her face, and her curly hickory-colored hair needed a proper wash.

Not exactly babe material. But apparently, that didn't matter to Mr. Seduction.

"And you are?" she prompted with a raised eyebrow.

His smirk widened at her gutsy reply, and he leaned against the porch beam, folding his arms across his chest. A zip-up gray hoodie covered his upper body, complete with the Robinson & Sons Roofing logo embroidered on the left side of the threadbare fabric. Dark-wash jeans perfectly hugged his firm thighs, and his boots were scuffed.

No pomp and circumstance with this man. Unfortunately, that only amplified his dangerous allure.

"Oh, I'm just the roofer," he drawled.

She tilted her head toward the door. "Well, they've started already. And I'm sure your boss won't appreciate your tardiness."

Amusement danced over his features. "Tardiness. My, my, my. You a teacher or something?"

The innocent question tugged at something deep within Mia. Once upon a time, that had been her dream. To be a music teacher like her grandmother. But destiny had other plans for her—plans that everyone insisted were more worthy of her extraordinary talent.

As if teaching wasn't a worthy calling. The implication still unsettled her spirit all these years later.

"No, I'm not a teacher," she answered, pursing her lips.

Mere minutes with this man, and she'd reverted from a thirty-seven-year-old woman into a cranky teenager. But when his attention returned to her mouth, she struggled to pull air into her lungs, and her annoyance evaporated as he licked his plump lips like he wanted to devour her for breakfast. The silence lengthened, tension brewing as the wind whistled and the water lapped on the rocks.

"You got a name?" he asked, the pitch of his voice impossibly deep.

"Sure do."

A husky laugh bubbled from his throat at her refusal to elaborate. Behind her, the screen door hinges squeaked, and she glanced back to see Eric the foreman. Relief washed over her that this seduction game would cease—mostly since she was a stone's throw away from bursting into flames.

"There you are," Eric said to the latecomer. "Wondered when Boss Man would show up."

Boss Man.

Mia's jaw dropped, and her head jerked back toward the unnamed man. He held her stare in a brazen challenge, daring her to say something. But shock rendered her unable to string a sentence together, and his eyes delivered a clear message.

Don't underestimate me.

His gaze remained on her as he answered Eric. "Got held up."

A splash of disappointment trickled through Mia when he broke their staring contest, stepped past her, and entered the house.

MAYBE I SHOULD GET *a hotel room for a few nights.*

The unreasonable thought tugged at her brain, her pride still wounded from the earlier encounter. But there was no point in wasting money if the home was perfectly livable, especially when Leslie had already texted with an update. After a full inspection, the crew estimated that the roof would take two days to repair, and then these men would be out of her life forever.

Surprisingly, Mia grew accustomed to the heavy hammering, the sound of power tools, and the men's colorful shouts from outside. After several days of total isolation, the cacophony was oddly soothing. But boredom persisted, and an itch to do something productive burrowed beneath her skin as the morning progressed. Instead of grabbing the blank manuscript sheet music still stuffed away in her luggage, she made a casserole.

Between the cardigan and the casserole, I really am channeling Granny.

The recipe had been a staple of her grandmother's kitchen and one of Mia's favorites growing up. Thankfully, the instructions were simple and straightforward, and her overwrought mind quieted as she got lost in the monotony of chopping broccoli, boiling chicken, and grating cheddar cheese. In the silence of the kitchen, Leslie's words skipped back into her brain.

"Get out of the city and focus on yourself for once. Rediscover your love of music. Make something great. You're way too fucking talented to let the last few years define your legacy."

A casserole probably wasn't what her agent had meant when she told Mia to make something great. But damn, she couldn't deny how good it felt to create something.

A light knock on the back door extracted her from the musings. "Come in," she called out, grabbing the potholder and removing the casserole from the oven.

The door squeaked open, and Eric stepped into the doorframe. "Just a heads-up that we're breaking for lunch."

"Oh. Well, if anyone's interested, I made this." She

pointed to the dish on the stovetop. "It should be edible. At least, I hope so."

"Hey, it's free," Eric replied with a laugh. "That's all we care about."

She barely had time to prepare a plate before they barreled into the kitchen like eager school children dismissed for recess. Hyperaware of the Boss Man's continued presence, since his truck remained in the driveway, she escaped down the hallway before he appeared, her bare feet skidding along the runner carpet.

Her distracted mind brought her to the parlor instead of the den, and her hands shook as she laid eyes on the gorgeous baby grand Steinway piano she'd been ignoring for days.

The immaculate instrument was polished to perfection. An absolute sight for sore eyes.

It made her sick to her stomach.

She was no stranger to pianos. From the light-up Fisher Price keyboard her grandmother had purchased for her first birthday to the Yamaha upright piano at her elementary school to the wide range of options at Juilliard—she'd mastered them all.

A prodigy, they'd called her. Maestro Mia. There wasn't a music award she hadn't won, wasn't a grand stage she hadn't performed upon to a sold-out audience. And then her passion project—the musical she and her ex-husband first brainstormed during their freshman year at Juilliard—went into previews off-Broadway. Over ten years of dedication and workshopping paid off. Buzz grew and interest increased, and it was fast-tracked to the Lunt-Fontanne as a certified smash hit. Before she knew it, they were household names. The next Rodgers and Hammerstein.

But the higher you rise, the harder you fall.

Because, despite the success and accolades, she couldn't bear to sit at the piano in a quaint beach house in Connecticut.

She should've course corrected to the den, but running scared from the big, bad piano was too pathetic to stomach. So she parked her tush on the love seat and tucked into her meal—*delicious. Granny would be proud*—while eavesdropping on the conversation in the other room. The men were a bunch of gossips, and she smiled at their lively chatter. Apparently, someone named Dennis Coates was rumored to be in poor health, although the family was trying to keep it hush-hush. Nothing quite like small-town life.

Once she finished her meal, she placed the empty plate to the side. The Steinway called to her like an old lover she no longer trusted.

Sit down. Start playing. You know what you're doing.

Peeved at her own foolishness, she stepped toward the bench and sat, her backside sinking into the plush leather cushion. An overwhelming sense of familiarity surrounded her, and a complicated mix of emotions lodged in her throat. If she didn't know any better, she could've sworn her grandmother stood behind her, wrapping her frail arms around Mia's shoulders. That small comfort provided enough fortitude to place her fingers on the keys, her foot following onto the sustain pedal.

But something prevented her from pressing down and letting the music flow.

"Do you play?"

An unladylike yelp burst into the air, and she almost jumped off the seat. Whirling around, she found Boss Man leaning against the doorframe, his stance the epitome of casual seduction, although true sincerity was laced into the question.

"Yes—no! I mean—can I help you with something?" she sputtered.

His tawny brows narrowed at her curtness. "We finished lunch. Loaded the dishwasher. Just wanted to let you know."

"Oh. Thank you."

She cringed internally at the unintentional haughtiness, his jaw clenching at her apparent dismissal. Instead of exiting in a huff, he grabbed her empty plate and, with one last weighted look, left the room. Soon after, the men's chatter faded, the screen door slamming as they returned to work.

Alone in the cottage, Mia fled the parlor, caught off guard by her reaction to the piano. Lord knows she wasn't ready to unpack every intense feeling—how the shiny ivories felt beneath her fingers or how her body had naturally melted into the bench's cushion.

But equally concerning was how a private part of her reveled at the idea of performing for the man who'd interrupted the intimate moment. Clearly, he considered her a stuck-up city girl, and she secretly wished to humble him with the force of her talent.

All the more reason to stay away from him.

Reality television was always a reliable distraction, so she headed to the den to rot her brain for several hours. A streak of sunlight filtered through the open blinds later that afternoon, illuminating the room and pulling her from a trashy TV coma. The persistent clouds of the past few days hadn't helped with her already downtrodden mood, so she rushed onto the porch to behold the warm glow.

The salty sea breeze whipped her curly tresses like a twister, and she propped her hip against the cedar porch railing, but the sun reflecting off the water didn't transfix her for long. The men were packing up for the day, and the tool kits crashing onto the flatbed stole her attention. Boss Man barked orders like a natural leader, but he wasn't afraid to get his hands dirty, evident in how he hauled the ladder atop the truck with ease.

From a distance, he almost looked ordinary. But the nape of her neck tingled when he caught her watching, and there was no mistaking the man's true nature. His powerful stare summoned a whirlwind of unrest in her, but she averted her gaze, keeping it on the water's horizon until the trucks departed.

TWO

The Daymont Tavern was one of the few establishments open year-round. Many of the restaurants and lounges lining the coast were seasonal, closing at the end of September and reopening in early May. But the Daymont Tavern—or the DT, as it was known by many—was the place for townies. Those in a certain socioeconomic bracket, at least. The wealthy locals imbibed at the Club House located in the exclusive members-only Daymont Yacht Club, but the working-class residents drank at the DT.

Since she lacked a guest pass to the yacht club, the DT was her only option for a night out. The roofing crew's departure had left her feeling strangely bereft, and cabin fever had commenced. Eager to get out for a while, she showered, dressed, and then drove the short distance over to the DT.

A compact and unassuming one-story brick building, the tavern contained a weathered green awning boasting the name and date established: *Daymont Tavern. Family owned and operated since 1919.* A battered sign announced more parking in the rear, but a lone spot was free up front. Mia parked her rental car and walked to the entrance.

Inside, the DT was no different from any other pub in America. Soft and soulful yacht rock played over the sound system, the tunes blending into the lively chatter. The bar was modest, with only ten rickety stools, and several high-top tables were indeterminately placed around the room. A pool table sat in the back right corner, with three dartboards affixed to the nearby wall. The floor was sticky, and the place smelled like fried food and cheap liquor, but an undeniable homelike quality filled the air.

Heads swiveled to appraise her where she stood at the entrance. Although she'd dressed down—jeans, slate-gray sweater, and white sneakers—she still stuck out like a sore thumb. This place catered to regulars, and she had *outsider* written all over her.

Her heart bounced frantically at the sight of one particular regular.

The roofer. Boss Man.

He stood at the dartboards with a buddy, his hoodie draped across the nearest high-top table. A plain black T-shirt encased his torso, and a tattoo peeked out from under the sleeve on his left arm, although she was too far away to decipher the design.

His eyes immediately found hers, but she deflected her gaze before the moment transformed into something more. Sadly, it wasn't quick enough to stop her libido from rearing its ugly head, and a dull throb emerged between her legs.

Focus, Mia. You're here for dinner and drinks, not roguish men and bad decisions.

Holding to that resolve, Mia sat at the bar. An older woman in her fifties was slinging drinks for customers.

Between her frizzy bleach-blond hair and leathered skin that hinted at a youth sans sunscreen, it was evident this woman was a no-nonsense broad. One perfectly penciled-on eyebrow rose as she approached Mia, throwing the food menu onto the sticky wooden bar top.

"You new around here?" the woman asked, pulling no punches.

"Just visiting."

"During this time of year?"

Mia nodded absently and craned her head to examine the beer selections. "Can you tell me what you have on tap?"

The bartender rattled off the options, and Mia ordered a hazy IPA from a local brewery. Perfectly chilled and deliciously juicy, the beer traveled down her throat with ease. After a glance at the food menu, she ordered the specialty flatbread topped with butternut squash and caramelized onions.

"Don't I know you from somewhere?" the woman asked, staring intently as Mia handed over the laminated menu.

A chill of unease coasted up her spine. It had been years since she'd granted on-camera interviews or attended any award shows, her social media had been scrubbed, and she'd flown under the radar since her last musical flopped. But at one time, her face had been everywhere. She'd been as famous as a composer could be in the modern era when the vast majority of the general public lauded auto-tuned earworms above all else.

Granted, she'd already experienced notoriety in the music industry, ever since first performing at Carnegie Hall at the tender age of seven. But this had been a different beast entirely. She went from being famous in a small, esoteric world—bridging the gap between classical composition and traditional musical theatre and modern musical sensibilities—to being *famous*, famous.

It was the kind of fame that sucked away one's true purpose—when people became interested in *her* rather than her art.

Her ex-husband had taken to the attention like a duck to water. Mia, not so much. It was no wonder the relationship deteriorated to the point of no return.

Gulping down the unpleasant memories, Mia shook her head. "I think I just have one of those faces."

That vague explanation satisfied the bartender, as she shrugged and went to shoot the shit with another patron.

Dodged a bullet. For now.

A large mirror mounted on the wall behind the bar gave Mia a full view of everything happening behind her, and—against her better judgment—her focus continually fell on the roofer. But she wasn't alone in her covert observance. His eyes also flickered toward her while he played darts, although she tried to dodge his stare as much as possible.

But she knew, deep down, that he'd meander over. They'd spar and flirt, and the tension between them would increase. Maybe if she'd been the Mia of years ago—freshly divorced and ready to jump on any man who looked her way—she'd be willing to entertain his blatant seduction. But today's Mia knew better than to let a charming flirt sweet-talk her out of her panties.

Although, it could be fun to knock him down a peg or two.

Dinner arrived a few minutes later, and she devoured the flatbread, savoring the explosion of flavors. Her plate was clean and her beer was nearly finished when Boss Man finally approached.

"Funny seeing you here," he murmured, slipping his well-formed arms back into his hoodie. Much to her chagrin.

Her gaze swung over to acknowledge him. "Why's that?"

Sculpted shoulders lifted into a nonchalant shrug. "Figured you'd be more interested in one of Daymont's finer establishments where cocktails cost twenty bucks a pop."

"Those places are closed for the season."

"You checked." A smug smirk appeared, accompanied by a touch of playfulness. "Thank you for proving my point."

She rolled her eyes in response, which only seemed to delight him further. His smirk morphed into a genuine grin, and his handsomeness nearly knocked her over. But it wasn't only his attractive physical features that captivated her—the man had presence. A vibrating sensuality that was impossible to ignore.

"Dee, can I get another?" he called to the bartender, holding up his empty glass. "And another for...?" Trailing off, he raised his brows and gestured toward her with unmistakable intent. He wanted her name, and surprisingly, she wanted to oblige.

With a conceding dip of her head, she answered, "Mia."

"Mia," he repeated, his delivery laced with suggestiveness.

She narrowed her eyes at him, but his silent comeback was a flirtatious wink. The bartender sighed with exhaustion as she placed two fresh beers on the bar.

"Travis Flynn, you better not bother this woman," Dee ordered in a stern voice.

His name raced through her veins, heating her blood like a firestorm. Or a lustful portent. Either way, their connection had now evolved into something more. First name basis. Acquaintances.

That fact did nothing to cool her down.

"Am I bothering you?" he asked Mia, a smidge of sincerity in the question.

She took a sip of beer, keen to make him wait. "Not yet."

Her succinct reply pulled a snort from Dee, who cleared the empty plate and headed to the kitchen without another word. Travis took a seat on the empty barstool beside Mia, turning his body toward her, his legs wide and welcoming. It took every ounce of fortitude to not look at his crotch.

"Dee's my godmother," he explained. "She likes to give me a hard time."

"I'm sure you deserve it."

He laughed, the sound as decadent as dark chocolate. "Can't argue with that."

Mia trailed one finger up the length of her glass, condensation wetting her skin. "Your name's not Robinson?" she asked, pointing to the logo on his hoodie.

"Nope. Cole Robinson was my mentor. I started working for him when I was eighteen, and he sold the company to me a few years back."

"Why didn't you change the name?"

"Because I learned everything I know from that man. He was like a father to me. I'm one of the sons in Robinson & Sons Roofing, whether it's my last name or not."

The sweet sentiment caught her by surprise. It also hinted at tension with his actual father, which piqued her interest, but she squashed the curiosity, suspecting that the more she learned about him, the more irresistible he'd become. Best to keep their discussions to surface-level topics only.

His strong throat bobbed as he gulped his beer, but she dragged her focus away before the sight hypnotized her. All for naught since she found his reflection, their eyes locking in the mirror behind the bar.

He held her gaze through the glass and asked, "What brings you to our little town?"

"Needed to get away for a while," she hedged with a shrug.

"Vacation?"

"Something like that."

"Odd time of year to visit. Most people summer in Daymont."

"Maybe I'm not a summer type of girl."

He broke the mirror connection and turned toward her, leaning closer. "Tell me what type of girl you are."

"I don't think you can handle that."

"Try me," he dared.

Flirting with a local townie wasn't the worst way to spend a few hours, but their sparring shouldn't have sent her into a tizzy. It wasn't only her physical reaction that gave her pause—how her nipples tightened and her core hummed—but more so how her chest swelled with a foolish, giddy desire.

Get a hold of yourself. You're too old to act like an infatuated schoolgirl.

"I assume you grew up here?" she asked, changing the subject.

"You assume right."

"Other than drinking here, any suggestions to keep me busy?"

"Oh, I can think of a few things."

As hard as she tried, Mia couldn't suppress her laughter. It tumbled from her mouth without pretense, a pure response to his utterly shameless answer. And he knew it, too, judging from his troublemaking grin.

"That was ridiculous," she choked out once the giggles subsided.

"Maybe. Worth it to hear you laugh, though."

The earnestness in his voice nudged her off kilter. She'd never met a man who moved so seamlessly from rapscallion to genuine gentleman, and it was difficult to grasp his real identity. What would it be like to peel back the layers of this man? Would she like what she saw?

Such questions could keep her up at night if she let them.

He gestured to the back of the bar. "Up for a game of pool?"

"Why do I feel like there'll be a wager involved?"

"Smart girl," he purred. "What do you say?"

"I'm not a betting woman," she said with a self-deprecating laugh.

At least she wasn't any longer. The one time she'd taken a chance in her career, it had flopped miserably. Arrogance had gotten the better of her. From now on, she'd walk the straight and narrow in every aspect of her life, whether personal or professional.

And this man was *not* the straight and narrow. He was a winding, twisting road to ruin.

Travis bit his lip in thought. "I'm not sure I believe that."

"Believe what you want. Besides, I should get going," she added after a quick glance at her watch.

"Ah, but the night is young."

"And I have to get up early." She gave him a knowing look. "My home will be invaded by a bunch of men before breakfast."

"Fair enough," he said with a bark of laughter.

She signaled for the bill, and Dee placed it on the bar in mere seconds, but Travis's hand shot out to snatch it first. Their hands brushed, and Mia sucked in a surprised breath at how natural the caress felt against her skin.

Unaffected by the minor graze, he reached into his back pocket for his wallet. "I got it."

"Oh, no you don't."

"Consider it thanks for lunch." He threw several bills down onto the folio. "Now we're even."

A wise move on his part, as she never would've permitted the liberty otherwise. The last thing she wanted was to be in debt to him. No doubt, one day, he'd come to collect. But since this made things even, she conceded with a weary nod.

When she stepped off the stool, he also rose to his feet. Almost as if they were a courting couple of yesteryears, and it was his duty to see her off properly. But it also meant that their bodies became unbearably close, caught between the tight quarters of the stools.

Thanks to her height of five eight, there was no need to tip her head back to look at him, although her heart skipped a beat at their close proximity. Clammy hands grabbed her purse, throwing it over her shoulder as she attempted to act natural.

Clearing her throat, she stepped back to create more space lest she plaster her ample body against his athletic frame in a moment of madness. "Thanks for dinner."

"You're welcome." He gave her a final once-over, leaning against the bar. "See you tomorrow."

Tomorrow hadn't meant much over the past few years. Another day of floundering, of feeling like a failure. Of not living up to the title bestowed upon her. But for the first time in a long time, the promise of tomorrow held weight. Her skin tingled as she departed the tavern, the heat of his gaze like an inevitable brand.

THREE

The crew arrived at eight sharp, soon after Mia chose an outfit. Pathetic that she spent twenty agonizing minutes trying to decide, but no one needed to know that but her. She kept it casual—another pair of jeans and a lightweight sweater—although the top's striking V-neck perfectly emphasized her breasts.

Travis Flynn was the definition of shameless. Why shouldn't she follow suit?

The Robinson & Sons Roofing pickup pulled into the driveway first, followed by Travis's sleek truck. She watched from the kitchen window, nibbling on a protein bar as fresh coffee trickled into the pot. Apparently, she was gunning for the title of Connecticut's Best Hostess, since she headed onto the porch with the pot and three mugs.

"Anyone want coffee?" she called out.

The guys nodded eagerly, while Travis's look suggested he was more interested in drinking *her* down.

"What's on the menu for lunch?" Eric joked as he poured himself a mug.

Conflicting emotions surged in her chest in response to the innocent question.

Am I so petrified of the piano that I've let myself be reduced to some 1950s housewife archetype?

Her feminist sensibilities bristled. But after languishing with nothing to do for days, making the casserole had given her a purpose—albeit a small one. Still, there was no denying that she was stuck in a rut of the worst kind if she preferred the role of merry homemaker instead of award-winning composer.

The Steinway called to her from inside the house, and her hands shook at memories of soft adagios and lively allegros. But instead of telling the men that they were on their own for lunch, she dug her head deeper into the sand.

"It's a surprise," she improvised. "I have to run to the market, though. Do you need access to the house?"

Eric and Jerry looked to Travis for an answer, but he shook his head silently. Not without a hint of a lustful smile, of course. With that settled, she grabbed her leather jacket and purse before locking up the cottage. The driveway was wide enough that their vehicles hadn't boxed in her rental car, and she started the journey to the nearest market.

Downtown Daymont was relatively sleepy for a Thursday morning. The wind persisted after the storm, and brittle leaves crunched under her boots as she strolled down the street. Several storefronts were open for year-round residents—the hardware store, the grocery, the bakery—and many were decorated for Halloween.

One building stopped Mia in her tracks.

Daymont Symphony School.

Music note decals populated the window, although their frayed condition hinted at a long history in town.

Music lessons for all ages and abilities! was imprinted between the musical embellishments, the font flourishing and evocative.

Pins and needles pricked her skin, but she forced her legs to move, ignoring the deep desire to introduce herself. Anonymity had become an anomaly, and it would be foolish to abandon something so rare. So she pushed the music school from her mind and entered the grocery store, focusing on the task at hand.

The crew was hard at work on the roof when she returned, but her nerves spiked at how Travis stomped around up there like he was invincible. As if one wrong move wouldn't put him out of commission completely. But at the same time, his recklessness was somehow incredibly attractive. That absence of fear. The drive to get the job done, no matter the circumstances.

Lust intertwined with distress in her stomach, a disconcerting combination she tried to shake off as she exited the car and grabbed the grocery bags.

Travis noticed her and called out, "Need a hand?"

"Nope, all good."

Once in the kitchen, she unloaded the ingredients into the fridge and pantry and then returned to the porch to retrieve the coffeepot and mugs from earlier. But Travis had already descended from the roof and beaten her to the punch.

"You taking a break already?" she quipped.

His devilish grin took center stage. "I'm the boss. I can do what I want."

"Is that right?" Holding out her hand for the coffeepot, she glowered when he didn't immediately hand it over.

Instead, his eyes dipped to admire her cleavage, and his

strong hand around the carafe's handle clenched. Her mind exploded with images of that same hand squeezing her breasts, and her nipples tightened at the fantasy. The taut buds were on full display due to her thin cashmere sweater, and his sinful mouth curled at the sight.

He extended the pot, and she reached for it, but the scoundrel had other ideas. With the handle in her grasp, he used the tenuous connection to pull her closer. A tiny gasp left her mouth as she stumbled forward, somehow stopping herself before colliding into his firm chest—as inviting as it looked.

"Whatcha making us for lunch?" he asked, not even attempting to hide the huskiness in his voice.

Tilting her head, she met his timbre with her own raspy reply. "You'll have to wait and find out."

"I like a woman who can cook, you know."

"Why doesn't that surprise me?" She stepped back, finally pulling the pot out of his hand. Sarcasm dripped from her words as she gestured toward him. "You give me I-want-my-woman-barefoot-and-pregnant-in-the-kitchen vibes."

He snorted, glancing away from her as his brows narrowed. "You think that little of me?"

"I don't know you. We only met yesterday, remember?" she reminded him.

A gust of wind brought a handful of errant leaves onto the porch, dancing around their feet. Silence swirled as Travis considered her words, keeping his gaze on the choppy water in the distance. The carved planes of his profile were as pretty as a picture, and a flash of fantasy invaded—the sight of that arresting face on a pillow beside her, both of them spent after a night of vigorous lovemaking.

His head turned, ensnaring her with a mischievous look as if he'd read her mind. "Oh, I remember."

Mia rolled her eyes to suppress the grin that wanted to escape. "Look, I appreciate the blatant flirting and all, but I'm thirty-seven. Way too old for bad boys."

"I like an older woman."

Her eyes widened in shock. "Wait, how old are you?"

"Thirty-five."

"Oh, give me a fucking break."

His hearty laugh weakened her knees. It wasn't fake or a product of his trifling persona. No, it was pure Travis, and every time he revealed that side of him, she desperately wanted to soak up more.

Her index finger pointed at him like a no-nonsense professor. "Get back to work."

He winked. "I like it when you boss me around."

Turning on her heel, she threw him a flirtatious look over her shoulder as she stepped into the house. "You say that now," she called back, the screen door slamming.

As morning turned into afternoon, the mouthwatering smell of chili filled the kitchen. Another recipe courtesy of her grandmother, and the perfect choice for a brisk autumn day. The spicy stew simmered until half past noon, and then Mia sounded the lunch call. Happy hoots echoed from the men, and they dashed through the back door several minutes later.

"Look at this," Eric remarked with delight. "You've got a whole setup."

Indeed she did. The pot of chili sat on the stove, a ladle on the counter nearby. Bowls were stacked beside a pile of spoons. Tiny serving bowls were filled with different toppings—shredded cheese, crushed tortilla chips, and sour cream. Freshly baked cornbread completed the conveyor belt of deliciousness.

"You've outdone yourself," Travis drawled from behind her.

Looking back, she almost swayed at his close proximity. He was near enough to lean back into his arms—top-tier arms contained in a long-sleeve navy-blue Henley that brought out his eyes. By now, she was no stranger to his blatant physicality, but it still affected her on a level she'd never experienced before.

Momentarily spellbound, she recovered quickly and replied with an unassuming shrug. "Just a bit of chili."

"So modest."

"Hush. Grab a bowl and eat."

With a laugh, Travis assembled his meal alongside his employees. They chattered together, an unmistakable sign of deep camaraderie. Mia hovered to the side until they sat at the kitchen table, and then she prepared her own bowl.

As she scooped the chili, it hit her that she wasn't simply hungry for food. What she craved more than anything was human connection. After being surrounded by people for ages—her ex-husband, friends, colleagues, adoring fans—much of her community had fallen by the wayside once she became persona non grata. And her grandmother's passing had been the ultimate blow.

Not to mention how the news of her ex-husband's romance with Broadway's biggest starlet—a woman twelve years his junior because *of course* he had to become a cliché—hit the papers the day of Granny's funeral.

It was no wonder Mia had turned into a shell of her former self. How she'd wound up in a cottage in Connecticut, surrounded by men she barely knew, wishing more than anything that they'd invite her to sit at the table and break bread with them.

Instead of awkwardly lingering, she snuck off to the parlor again and ate her lunch alone. The longer she remained in the room, the more she knew this stalemate with the Steinway couldn't last forever. She ran her fingers over the glossy top of the piano and inhaled a fortifying breath.

You can do this, Mia.

"I think I have some competition."

This man really has a habit of catching me in vulnerable moments.

Peeking behind her, she laid eyes on the perfect picture of temptation. He once again leaned against the doorframe, arms folded over his chest and ankles crossed, the toe of his work boot balanced against the hardwood floor. Her belly flip-flopped, but at least the reason for that reaction was this magnetic man and not the faultless instrument beside her for once.

"Competition?" she repeated.

"The way you're looking at that piano could make a guy jealous."

She scoffed. "Don't be ridiculous."

"Ah, but I'm so good at it."

That pulled a laugh from her, and his vibrant eyes sparkled at her reaction. He sat on the piano bench, with his back against the keys, and in the easy silence, Mia attempted to parse out her attraction to him. There was the obvious, of course. The handsome features, the sculpted arms, the undeniable charisma.

But there was something else about Travis that spoke to her, and the quiet epiphany was so simple it brought a bemused smile to her face. Because the truth was that she felt wonderfully normal with him. Just a woman attracted to a man. Both of them stripped down to their most basic identities. Maestro Mia didn't exist here, and that freedom was like walking on air.

"Do you, uh—" she started, her voice weak from the realization. Collecting herself, she forced out the question. "Do you play?"

"Nah. Don't have a musical bone in my body. You should've seen me playing the recorder in elementary school."

Mia chuckled at the thought of tiny Travis wreaking havoc on the woodwind. "Oh, I can imagine."

"Even if I wanted to play, this sort of thing was reserved for a certain section of Daymont." He sent her a speaking glance. "Fancy shit, you know?"

Her head dipped in a silent nod of understanding. It was a great injustice that the arts were often only accessible to the affluent, and Mia was fully aware of how she was living proof. Even if she hadn't found fame and fortune as a composer, she still never would've wanted for anything. She'd had money the second she was born, her family's wealth going back generations.

Sometimes, she wondered if her musical talent would've been nurtured if she'd been born to a different family. If she would've soared to such heights if a fat wallet hadn't been behind her. It was sobering to ponder how many untapped artistic geniuses were out in the world, forever undiscovered because of their financial circumstances.

And, as always, she thought of her beloved granny, a tenured professor at the Manhattan School of Music, who'd found an even higher purpose when she retired and began volunteering as a music teacher at after-school programs in disadvantaged neighborhoods.

Her grandmother had taught her many things. But the most important lesson she bestowed was that art was universal and should be accessible to everyone, no matter what.

The memories dissipated when Travis turned toward the piano keys. His roughened hands were a jarring juxtaposition to the piano's elegance, but the contrast was profoundly beautiful. And when his long index finger pushed and played a single note, the sound whisked through the room like an enchantment.

Just like that, her entire body vibrated with an overwhelming desire to play. To sit down and create music. To get lost in the beauty of the chords, the melodies, and the magic. But, even more so, she yearned to confide in him about the things most important to her.

"My grandmother was a music teacher. She taught me how to play," she whispered.

Travis tipped his head to find her gaze. "You any good?"

Amusement tugged at her lips. "I'm okay, I guess."

"Better than me, I'm sure." He played some random chords before halting the amateur performance with a sobering look. "You said she *was* a music teacher...did she pass?"

"Few years ago."

Compassion brimmed in his eyes. "I'm sorry."

She softly nodded her thanks. Death was a part of life, and her grandmother had lived a long and fulfilling one, but that didn't lessen the pain. While time helped dull the pang of her absence, Mia often wondered how she would've weathered the past few years if Granny had still been around to be her core support system.

"You think your grandmother would've liked me?" he asked coyly.

Mia threw him a teasing glare and said, "I still don't even know if *I* like you."

His hand shot to his chest, clutching his heart as if mortally wounded. Another laugh flew out of her, and he lit up at her reaction. He watched her intently, almost as if memorizing every laugh line on her face, documenting the ones he had created. Like he wanted to leave a mark on her.

"She did appreciate a charming man," she conceded with a good-natured smile.

"Ah, you two had that in common."

"Don't push it."

Now it was his turn to chuckle, but once the laughter died down, silence rippled between them. The air grew heavy, and a sensation swept over Mia—the reckless danger of teetering on the edge of a cliff.

Or perhaps a roof.

"We're on schedule to finish today," he told her in a hush.

She blinked a few times to refocus. "Hmm?"

"The roof. We'll finish it up today."

"Oh." She tried to gulp down the news as if it meant nothing. As if the thought of never seeing him again didn't cut her to the quick.

The intensity of his stare deepened. "Just thought you should know."

Then he stood, his wonderfully lean body unfolding to its full height. As the significance of his statement lingered, he grabbed her empty bowl and spoon and left the room without another word.

Fierce longing speared her as he departed, and she followed like a bat out of hell. But he reached the kitchen before she could stop him, and she schooled her features, mindful of Eric and Jerry.

Travis passed the bowl and utensil to Jerry, who was on dishwasher duty. Mia didn't even note Eric's absence until he reentered the cottage with an uneasy look, holding something close to his chest.

"I'm sorry to ask this," he began, "but would you mind signing my daughter's playbill?"

Her world tilted off its axis at the sight of the weathered booklet in his hand. Staring in shock, she clutched the counter to anchor herself, the cold marble a shock to her system. There was no denying it—her cover was blown, and her throat strained to form a reply.

So much for anonymity.

"Um. Sure."

Not the most eloquent or enthusiastic response, but it was something. To avoid Travis's probing look, she rummaged around for a marker.

"You famous or something?" Travis asked, the question fraught.

"No," she insisted in as firm a voice as she could muster. "Not at all."

Eric refuted that claim almost immediately. "You've never heard of Maestro Mia?"

"Guess I've been out of the loop," Travis answered in a clipped manner.

To her horror, Eric launched into an abridged version of her career. Completely disoriented, she continued searching for a marker as the words buzzed in her ears like white noise. One was stuffed in the back of a drawer, and her hands shook as she retrieved it and signed the playbill's front cover. She pushed the booklet into Eric's hands, stopping the Maestro Mia history lesson before he reached the most embarrassing portions of her story.

After avoiding Travis's gaze for as long as possible, she glanced at him with contrite eyes. Despite having nothing to apologize for, her chest still ached with regret. More than anything, she lamented the loss of the precious normalcy she'd experienced with him. Such fleeting moments, and she should've known it wouldn't last, but it didn't lessen the blow of the unmistakable despondency in his eyes. His expression confirmed that she'd morphed from a hoity-toity city girl he'd enjoyed teasing to something unattainable, and her head pounded painfully at the new reality.

Travis raised his eyebrows. "Sounds pretty famous to me."

"I'm not famous," she repeated. Trying to regain control of the situation, she turned to Eric. "Did you know the whole time?"

"You looked familiar, but it didn't hit me until last night," he explained. "I'm sorry to ask, but my daughter is a huge fan of the show, and she's been having a hard time at school lately—"

"It's fine," she said, cutting him off. He'd let the cat out of the bag in the worst way possible, but she couldn't begrudge him for being a good father. "But could you keep this under wraps? I'm trying to—"

"Stay anonymous?" Travis supplied.

Her eyes cut over to him in a silent plea to let sleeping dogs lie, at least for the time being. He could give her hell later, once she'd fully processed her loss of anonymity, and she tried to say as much to him without speaking a word.

"I won't say anything," Eric promised. "Thank you so much. This is going to make her day. You have no idea."

She permitted a tight smile and then tossed the marker back in the drawer. "I should start cleaning up."

"And we should get back to work," Travis added, eager to break up the awkward interval.

The men headed to the door, and Eric clasped Travis on the shoulder. "Still can't believe you stuck it out with us."

Although the comment wasn't intended for her, Mia jerked her head in surprise. "What do you mean?"

Eric nudged his boss in the side. "This one typically just checks in and then heads back to the office. He hasn't spent this much time on a worksite in God knows how long."

Travis scoffed, his cheeks turning pink. Mumbling under his breath, he stepped outside, and the other men left as well, leaving Mia alone to digest the news.

He stuck around for me.

Her eyes got misty at the revelation. Over the past few years, many people in her life had jumped ship when things got tough. Her ex-husband hadn't put up a fight to save their marriage, and her friends in the industry had stopped calling once her influence waned. Lord knows her parents were already aloof and distant and had been for her entire life. Otherwise, they may have ditched her too.

But *this* man, who she'd known for mere hours, had deviated from his routine in an effort to stay close.

Call her a sucker, but that detail sent her heart soaring into outer space, taking her common sense with it.

She cleaned the kitchen, packing the leftovers in a giddy daze, and eventually headed back to the parlor. The piano hadn't changed a bit, but it somehow looked different now. Like less of a threat. In truth, she still wasn't ready to play, but she sat on the bench in silence for what felt like hours and knew that she *would* play again one day soon.

Later that afternoon, a man's voice called from a

distance, accompanied by a knock on the back door. She practically skipped to the kitchen, eager to set the record straight with Travis.

But it was Eric on the other side of the screen door.

"We're all set here," he told her with a kind smile. "We'll reach out to Leslie to settle things, but you won't have to entertain our ugly mugs again. And thanks again for the playbill. I really do appreciate it."

She waved away his gratitude. "Of course. Is, um..."

But as her gaze darted to the driveway, the question got lost in her throat. Because Travis's truck was gone.

FOUR

Later that evening, indignation surged through her veins.

"Can you believe he didn't say goodbye?" she grumbled, pacing back and forth. Turning to the Steinway, she gestured wildly. "How dare he? The spineless bastard."

The piano didn't reply, being an inanimate object and all, and it occurred to Mia that she'd been ranting at the baby grand for the past five minutes.

Further proof she'd completely lost her head over Travis Flynn.

A part of her wanted to forget every charged moment they had shared. After all, the roof was fixed. He was out of her life forever, and in a few weeks' time, she'd head back to New York. Best to write the whole thing off as heavy flirtation and nothing more.

Unfortunately, her competitive nature roared to life. They'd started something, and she wasn't one to admit defeat, so she considered her options. An easy internet search would produce the contact information for Robinson & Sons Roofing, but there was another card to play.

The DT.

With a plan in place, she changed her outfit—*yes, I'm still pathetic, thanks for asking*—and jumped in the car, bound for Daymont's reliable watering hole. When she pushed through the door, the same scene welcomed her. The regular patrons, Dee behind the bar, and the smell of chicken wings and hot sauce perfuming the air.

Travis sat alone at the bar, nursing a beer without a care in the world. His quintessential smirk emerged as she crossed the threshold, and he tipped his beer to her in greeting. She glared without pretense, the sting of his Irish exit riling up her petty side.

Nothing better than an outfit change to assist in raking someone over the coals. The midi skirt she wore was a modest length, but the insanely long slit hit at mid-thigh. His jaw sagged at each exposed pop of her skin as she sauntered over. And goddamn it, she added a healthy dose of sway to her hips for good measure.

Take that, Boss Man.

Although his throat rippled, he recovered fast and arched a brow once she reached him. "Took you long enough," he declared.

She lifted herself onto the stool and sighed wearily. "Oh, shut up."

He laughed and passed the menu over. Dee asked for her drink order, wary eyes bouncing back and forth between them.

"Same as yesterday," Mia said.

Quick as a flash, Dee slammed an IPA down on the bar and made herself scarce.

Travis snorted. "Think we scared her?"

She expelled an amused puff of breath. "I can't imagine we're the worst she's dealt with."

"You say that now."

"Wanna split something?" she asked, motioning to the menu. "I have to eat, otherwise this beer will hit me like a ton of bricks."

"You like wings?"

"I do."

"Dee, we'll take an order of lemon-pepper wings," he called out to her. Then he addressed Mia, keeping his voice low as if revealing a massive secret. "The buffalo is good, but lemon pepper is superior."

She grinned. "Whatever you say."

A satisfied purr rumbled from his chest, and he found her gaze in the mirror behind the bar. Mia took a large gulp of her beer, relishing the juicy flavor profile. The chilled liquid helped cool her body for a few seconds, and she wondered whether to address the unspoken issue or ignore it completely.

He raised the topic before her. "I googled you."

With a groan, she plopped the beer down and covered her face with her hands. "Don't tell me that."

"A Pulitzer Prize, huh?"

"Don't."

"*I'm okay, I guess,*" he said in a poor imitation of her claim from earlier that day.

"Don't!"

His laughter masked an undercurrent of disillusionment in his demeanor. Catching his eye in the mirror again, she scrunched her face with reticence, and she offered an olive branch.

"I'm sure you also read about my fall from grace, too," she murmured.

"A bit," he admitted. "Your ex sounds like a prick."

Concise and to the point, as seemed to be his way. An

appreciative smile curled her lips, and the urge to confide in him deepened.

"I know I'm better off. It's just..." Pausing, she pondered how to sum up such a formative relationship. "He wasn't only my life partner. He was also my musical partner. We worked so well together, literally since the moment we met at Juilliard."

Travis whistled through his teeth. "Fancy."

"Don't," she warned again, this time in a more humorous manner. He held up his hands in surrender, and she continued. "My identity became so interwoven with him, both personally and professionally."

"So it must've stung when your first project without him wasn't, uh...well received."

"How diplomatic of you." After directing a look of gratitude his way, she spoke the harsh truth. "It was a spectacular flop. Twenty-five previews and only one performance before it closed. The papers ripped me to shreds. 'Maestro Mia's Massive Misstep,'" she said, reciting a memorable headline.

"Rude. But nice alliteration on their part."

"Yeah, even I had to give them props for that one."

They laughed together as Dee popped over with their wings, the savory aroma making Mia's stomach growl. Travis passed her an appetizer dish and a stack of napkins, and they piled their respective plates with chicken.

"The whole thing was doomed from the start," Mia reflected, still heavy with memories.

"Your marriage?"

"The musical. I rushed everything. The new lyricist I worked with? He and I didn't have time to get to know each other. To learn the other's quirks and processes. But the pressure to perform was breathing down my neck. To come out of the relationship as the winner, you know?"

His perfectly straight teeth pulled apart a wing, and he chewed thoughtfully. "There's always gotta be a winner."

"And I let that compromise my integrity. Because the truth is, sometimes great art takes time. You shouldn't rush it. And I forgot that." She bit into the chicken and then moaned. "Holy shit, this is good."

"Told you," he quipped. Then he wiggled his eyebrows. "I like that moan of yours."

"Shut *up*," she insisted with a laugh.

Their eyes met again in the mirror, and she almost swooned at his boyish grin, elated that things were back to normal after the Maestro Mia reveal. Here was proof that she was still a regular girl he could drink a beer with, Pulitzer Prize or not.

Travis tossed a picked-clean wing onto his plate. "Well, since we're sharing relationship woes, I'll raise your messy divorce with being left at the altar."

Her head whipped toward him so quickly, she almost broke her neck. "*What?*"

Ironically, he raised his beer in a toast. "Cheers to that, right?"

"Jesus, Travis. I hope she doesn't live in town, because I'd give her a piece of my mind."

"Nah, she's up in Boston now. Honestly, it would've ended in disaster anyway. I just wish the whole thing hadn't been so..." He hesitated, searching for the word. "Public."

"I know the feeling," she murmured, sending him a meaningful stare through the looking glass.

"I guess you do," he acknowledged faintly. Now that the floodgates were open, honesty flourished from him. "I was already the embarrassment of my family. The bride not showing up certainly didn't improve my reputation."

Confusion filled her. "Embarrassment? Why's that?"

"Ah, the curse of being the second son. My older brother is the golden boy. Always has been, always will be."

As an only child, Mia didn't understand sibling dynamics firsthand, but she could imagine how easily tension could arise if one constantly exceeded expectations. In fact, she wagered that if she had had a sibling, they likely would've hated her guts.

Although an apparently tense topic for him, she was hungry to uncover more. "What's your brother do?"

"Does he own his own business like yours truly? Sure doesn't. He works at the Daymont Yacht Club like every single member of my family has since the place first opened eight hundred million years ago. But *he worked his way up*," he recited in an unmistakable imitation of his family members. "Started as a dockhand in high school, and now he's Director of Waterfront Operations. La dee fucking da."

"Not that you're bitter or anything."

"No, of course not."

The immediate agreement was so comical that she snickered, and even Travis permitted a laugh. Shaking his head, he focused on his beer and inhaled deeply. Compassion twinged her chest as the truth behind his personality dawned. His roguish attitude was a product of his upbringing, of always being in the shadow of another person. He'd learned at a young age that acting up guaranteed attention—even if it wasn't the positive kind—and that conditioning followed him into adulthood.

"The same day I closed the deal with Cole to take over the roofing business was the day Thomas was promoted to director." The confession was soft, as if he'd never spoken this truth to anyone before. "And who do you think was celebrated that night?"

"I'm sorry," she offered in a whisper.

He wiped his hands with a napkin and tossed it onto the bar with a shrug. "Yeah. Well, you know what they say. You can pick your nose, but you can't pick your family."

The walls were back up, and Mia knew better than to continue pushing. "How eloquent."

With a suggestive stare, Travis leaned in closer. "Oh, you have no idea how eloquent I can be."

"Can you stop being a pervert for two seconds?"

"Not where you're concerned, baby."

Such a cheesy endearment should've made her balk in horror. *Baby* was an effortless pet name—smarmy and disingenuous if uttered by the wrong person. Travis, however, was exactly the right man to bestow such a term of affection. Her nipples tightened into hard peaks and arousal pooled between her legs, and she decided then and there that she'd take *baby* over *maestro* any day of the week.

But her competitiveness reemerged, with a determination to give as good as she got. Placing her index finger in her mouth, she sucked the dry rub seasoning from her skin, keeping her gaze on him the entire time. His icicle eyes flashed with lust at the brazen display.

The finger left her mouth with a *pop*, and she smiled innocently. "Delicious."

"Evil," he whispered, drawing the word out for emphasis.

"Oh, for Christ's sake," Dee muttered at the other end of the bar.

Try as they might to squash their laughter, a fit of giggles commenced. Sure, they were full-blown adults, but being with Travis made her feel no different from a carefree teenager. Even still, Mia couldn't justify more finger licking, so she stepped off the stool for a bathroom break.

"That's not a bad idea," he agreed, motioning for her to go first. "You want another beer?"

"Sure. And a water too."

She headed to the restroom with an extra pep in her step. While washing her hands, the cold water against her red-hot skin a welcome reprieve, she glanced at herself in the mirror. A heap of warm-brown curls framed a face brimming with reckless delirium, hazel eyes that were once hollow now shined with zest, and a healthy pink flush tinted her normally pale skin.

Amazing how some spirited flirting could completely transform a girl.

Walking on air, she retraced her steps to the bar and side-stepped Travis with a playful salute as he ambled to the hallway housing the unisex bathrooms. She chugged some water and sought to get her heart rate under control while he was gone, but that endeavor went out the window when he returned with a come-hither grin.

"Let's play a game," he said, nodding to the pool table at the back of the tavern.

As if they hadn't been doing that since the instant they'd met. His calloused palm extended in an obvious invitation, and she didn't hesitate to place her hand in his, allowing him to lead her toward the billiard table.

"You play at all?" he asked, grabbing two cue sticks from the rack built into the wall.

She placed her beer on the corner of the table and took the cue stick from him with a sheepish glance. "Not really."

"Excellent."

"I already know what you're thinking. You wanna give me a full tutorial, right? Bend me over the table and teach me how to hold this thing properly?" she prompted with a nod to the stick.

"Only if you're into that."

Rolling her eyes, she waved her hand back and forth. "Rack the balls."

A growl rumbled from his chest, but he obeyed her command and prepped the table for their game. "Still not a betting woman?"

"Depends on the wager."

"Loser has to answer a question. Any question the winner asks. And they have to be brutally honest."

An intriguing proposition. They'd already engaged in one session of brutal honesty, and she couldn't pass up the chance for more.

"Deal," she said, holding her hand out for a shake.

He clasped their palms together and used the physical connection to tug her closer, no different from his stunt earlier that day. "Good luck."

After one strong shake, Mia pulled away and placed her hand on her hip. "Thanks, Boss Man."

That nickname had a different connotation coming from her, and his eyes turned dark with incendiary heat. But before things escalated, he gave her the honor of first strike, and the cue ball smacked into the colored globes. They flew to every corner of the table, and Mia considered her options before sinking the solid red ball into the top right pocket with a straight shot.

"I thought you didn't play," Travis remarked with a suspicious glance.

"I don't," she chirped. "I just really love winning."

With the gauntlet officially thrown, they traded plays over the next forty-five minutes, their competitiveness intensifying with each move. Teasing barbs were exchanged, laughter was contagious, and in the end, she won fair and square.

Travis took the defeat in stride, bestowing her with a courtly bow. "Well done. Go ahead, do your worst. Ask me anything."

Dozens of questions flashed through her mind. She leaned her right hip against the billiard table, placed the cue stick onto the ground for leverage, and studied him. Eventually, one question won out.

"Why didn't you say goodbye today?"

His sandy brows knit together, and he blatantly avoided her searching gaze. "Didn't think you'd notice."

"Bullshit."

Her reply was hushed but vehement enough that he pinned her with a stare so powerful she almost gasped. The rest of the tavern faded into a blur as she waited for his answer. Waited for the truth.

"I thought it would make it easier to forget about you," he eventually admitted.

Her breath caught in her chest, but she managed to choke out a reply. "Did it?"

"Fuck no."

All the oxygen was sucked out of the room. His confession completely consumed her, and all her defenses crumbled to the ground.

"I'm going back to New York in a few weeks," she said, struggling to keep her voice steady.

He nodded slowly. "That's probably a good thing."

"Yeah. It probably is."

The moment lingered, coiling and twisting and transforming into an unspoken agreement.

This was inevitable. They both knew that. But it would be casual. Nothing more, nothing less.

"You wanna get out of here?" he asked.

Her shaky nod was all he needed to beeline back to the bar and settle their tab with Dee. Mia didn't bother fighting to split the cost, knowing he wouldn't hear of it.

Dee, bless her, didn't say a word as Travis signed the credit card receipt. But before exiting the tavern, he glanced over his shoulder to ensure the coast was clear before tugging Mia down the hallway leading to the bathrooms.

"Where are we going?"

"I'm sure you'll give me shit for this later, but I don't care. I can't wait another fucking second."

And then he pushed her against the wall and kissed her.

FIVE

His lips were a sin, and she was bound for hell.

Mia moaned as his large hands invaded her body, moving from her hips to her backside with finesse. The man talked a good game, but he wasn't all talk. This supreme flirt had the kissing skills to match, and each drag of his lips against her own unleashed a tidal wave of passion within her.

With her back wedged against the wall, she trailed her hands up his muscular arms, relishing the feel of his strong form. An animalistic noise filled her ears when she dug her fingernails into the fabric of his hoodie, and he thrust his hips forward in a beautifully brazen manner. Heat bolted through her like a devastating lightning strike, the grinding of his rigid length against her belly further fanning the flames. Her senses went into overdrive, and she inhaled his scent—a faint hint of cedarwood mixed with his natural male musk.

Travis, Travis, Travis, Travis echoed in her mind. An erotic hymn. But once air became essential, she broke away from the kiss and heaved a deep breath. He showered her neck with frantic pecks before nipping at the flesh with his teeth. The sharp sting pulled a gasp from her chest, the touch of pain sending another flood of arousal to her aching pussy.

"Bad," she chastised playfully.

"Yeah." He moved away from her neck to find her eyes. "And you like it."

No point denying the truth. After a quick nod, she grasped his jaw and pulled him in for another red-hot kiss. Deft strokes of his tongue splintered her self-control, and the quivering in her core became too much to bear. She widened her stance and hooked one leg around him, indifferent to how her skirt hitched up, then rubbed her needy center against his jean-clad, muscled thigh.

"Fuck." The expletive hissed against her neck, and he pulled back to watch her pelvis move against him. "That's it. Show me how much you fucking need it, baby."

Her arousal soared to another height as she gyrated against his sturdy limb, amplified by how he watched her movements with the perfect combination of passion and reverence—as if imagining her straddling him and moving in the same manner. But her shameless dry hump didn't last long, because footsteps snapped them out of the carnal haze. The reality of their location reared its ugly head, and she quickly placed her leg down.

"Someone's coming," she whispered.

A mischievous grin stretched across his face, and he pulled her into one of the nearby restrooms. Stumbling through the door, she caught herself on the side of the single stall. As she got her bearings, Travis closed the door behind them, the heavy *snick* of the deadbolt promising debauchery.

"Someone's coming, you say?" he teased.

A soft laugh sprang from her. "This is crazy."

"*You* make me crazy."

His large hands trembled as they seized her hips, his wicked mouth finding hers once again. With their tongues dueling for dominance, his grip traveled beneath her skirt, and a fervid groan echoed the second he grasped her bare thigh.

"Lift it," he ordered.

Mia would've balked at such a command on any other day with any other man. But not this time. Without hesitation, she gathered her skirt and pulled it above her waist. Since she hadn't planned for a torrid tryst, she wore a simple cotton thong, but judging from the heat in his gaze, she could've been clad in the most titillating lingerie for all he cared.

"Are you wet?" Travis asked in a low voice.

The question was a no-brainer, but she tilted her pelvis toward him in invitation. "See for yourself."

His hand shot forward and cupped her mound, a deep growl rumbling as he caressed the damp fabric. A gasp caught in her throat, the sound building to a cry when two fingers pointedly pushed against her clit.

"Shh." Softening the chastisement, he leaned in for a quick kiss. "We can't have anyone interrupting us, can we?"

She shook her head. "I'll be quiet."

But when his fingers breached the fabric and trailed through the curls above her core to make contact with her pussy, that promise became arduous. Especially since he kept running his mouth, pushing her buttons with each filthy word.

"Ah, fuck. You're drenched. Listen to that." He skimmed his fingers through her folds, the sopping sound of her arousal unmistakable. "I can literally fucking hear it."

"Travis, please," she panted.

"Hmm?"

"*Please.*"

"Please, what?" he prompted.

Infuriating man. I'll make him pay for this.

Until then, she had no choice but to beg. "My clit. Harder. Please."

"Why the rush, baby?"

She gritted her teeth and seethed, "Because we're in a goddamn public restroom, and I haven't had sex in months, that's why."

Finally, his fingers found the bundle of nerves and applied pressure. She bit her bottom lip to suppress a moan, her head falling to rest on his shoulder as he rubbed firm circles against her clit.

He clucked his tongue in disapproval. "Months, huh? Poor thing."

"Don't start."

A husky laugh answered her before he suddenly switched their positions. Her skirt dropped when he whirled her around, plastering the front of his body against her back. They locked eyes in the mirror over the sink, and the reason for this adjustment somehow registered in her lust-addled brain.

A seductive command tickled her ear. "Watch us."

Like at the bar, the looking glass offered a deeper level of connection. It was a tool to pull back their layers. To create cracks in their facades. To strip them both bare.

Not to mention it was hot as hell, and she shivered at the prospect of watching him work her over.

"Mind that skirt," he whispered.

She devised a quick solution, tucking the bottom of the skirt into her waistband to keep her hands free.

He raised an impressed eyebrow. "How resourceful."

Instead of burrowing his hand beneath her panties again, he guided the fabric down her trembling legs. Grateful for his steady form behind her, she stepped out of them and then gasped when he hooked his elbow behind her right knee and placed her foot on the lid of the wastebasket, fully exposing her pussy in the mirror.

It was obscene.

She loved it.

His index finger teased her slickness, brushing over her clit before lightly tapping it. The visual in the mirror, coupled with the soft pats against her sensitive bud, drove her wild. Then two fingers plunged deep, stretching her tightness, and she thrashed with abandon.

"Oh fuck," she cried out, her heart knocking against her ribs. "Oh fuck, Travis."

"Quiet, baby," he murmured.

"Cover my mouth."

His brows knit together as his eyes found hers in the mirror. "You sure?"

"Unless you want this entire bar to hear me scream," she warned him through clenched teeth. "*Cover my mouth.*"

He obliged, placing his free hand atop her kiss-swollen lips, and she moaned ruthlessly against his skin. Muffled keens increased as she watched his broad fingers thrust in and out of her, his thumb working her clit with finesse.

"Fuck, you're creaming my hand like crazy." His husky laugh brushed her ear, and then he took the lobe between his teeth and tugged. "You fucking sexy girl."

Desperate for more of him, she slanted her pelvis and rubbed her ass against his straining erection. A guttural sound vibrated from his torso.

"Yeah, I know, baby," he grunted. "We'll get there. But

first, you're gonna come for me. Then I'm taking you back to that cottage and fucking you so hard you won't be able to think straight."

As if she could think straight now. But that filthy promise took her over the edge, her climax slicing through her body. It cleaved her in two—before Travis and after Travis—and her core convulsed with powerful pulses while she sobbed with pleasure against his hand.

Slowly, she came back down to earth, and Travis gently released his grip. Cold porcelain cooled her skin as she clutched the side of the sink, her heavy pants filling the air as they focused on each other in the mirror. He held her stare as he brought his hand—the one that had brought her to heaven and back—to his mouth, his wicked tongue licking the fingers clean.

His lips twisted into the sexiest smile she'd ever seen, and a simple question fell from them.

"Ready to go?"

THE DRIVE BACK WAS PAINFUL.

For one thing, she wasn't wearing panties. Travis had stuffed them into his back pocket, and she couldn't muster any energy to comment on his trophy. Instead, she set herself to rights, and they separately exited the bathroom in the hopes of keeping a low profile.

She'd kept her eyes on her feet and rushed through the exit, knowing she could never show her face at the DT again.

Worth it.

And so she drove back to the cottage, panty-less and punch-drunk with lust. Headlights cut through the sheath of night as she traveled toward the coast, her inner muscles still fluttering with mild pulses. Almost as if they were calling to Travis. And he was right on her heels, his truck trailing at an absurdly close distance.

The roads were clear, so she pulled into the driveway in record time. A sliver of light from the waxing crescent moon shone down on her as she exited the car and ascended the porch steps. The slam of a car door caught her attention, and Travis's formidable form cut through the darkness like a man on a mission.

"Nice tailgating," she quipped to lighten the mood.

His gaze dipped to her ass as he scaled the steps. "You better get that door open."

A piercing statement. A warning that he'd be more than willing to fuck her out on the porch in the moonlight if he had to wait one more minute. Certainly a thrilling scenario, but she unlocked the back door nevertheless.

Entering the kitchen, she tossed her purse onto the counter and toed off her shoes. "Get your shirt off."

"Bossy," he joked, closing the door with a wry glance.

But he heeded her command and unzipped the Robinson & Sons Roofing hoodie, then dragged the T-shirt up over his head. Her eyes raked over his beautiful upper body of strong muscles and sturdy sinew, and the space between her thighs hummed at the dusting of dark-bronze hair covering his pectorals. The masculine tufts trailed down his sculpted abdominals and disappeared into his jeans, and her hands itched with the need to strip him completely nude.

He raised an eyebrow. "You gonna join me? Because if you knew how often I've thought about that body of yours, you wouldn't keep me waiting."

But before she could undress, something caught her eye

—the tattoo on his left bicep. In the darkness of the room, she squinted to study the design, focusing on the word inked into his skin.

Flynn.

With an outstretched hand, she rubbed her fingers against the vibrant colors of the tattoo. Along with his surname, there was a blue pendant that contained a silver medieval helmet and a proud wolf, the entire design flanked by swirls of gold.

"Is this your family crest?" she asked in a whisper.

He cleared his throat in an attempt to sound indifferent. "Coat of arms, technically."

Despite the nonchalant answer, the correction was proof that he cared. Even with the grievances he'd shared earlier, Mia knew this man loved his family something fierce and craved their acceptance more than anything in the world.

Leaning down, she placed a soft kiss against the ink. "I like it."

A strangled sound shuddered from his chest, and he stood still as stone for a handful of seconds. Evidently, tender shows of affection were uncommon for him, and her heart warmed at his stunned expression. But the pitter-patter of her pulse increased when he gripped her hips and pulled her closer, wedging her back against the counter.

"Oh yeah?" he rumbled. "What else you like?"

With a throaty laugh, she fused their lips together and savored how his lean body perfectly pressed against her soft curves. Her nipples were painfully hard, and she rubbed the buds against his firm chest. In tune with her needs, he tore his mouth away to pull her sweater above her head, tossing it aside. Electricity sparked in her core when he grasped her breasts, kneading the flesh and tweaking the taut peaks through her cotton bra, and the clank of his belt buckle unfastening made her pussy further clench in anticipation.

He pushed his snug jeans down and then did an awkward dance to unlace and remove his boots. Clad in only gray boxer briefs, he suddenly bent down, giving himself enough leverage to throw her over his shoulder. She thrashed against him in confusion as he moved out of the kitchen.

"What are you—" A firm smack on her backside shocked her silent for a second. Until she yelped, "Did you just slap my ass?"

"Sure did. Stop squirming."

"You're insane."

"Keep insulting me, baby. You know it gets me riled up."

She huffed out an indignant breath—although her lips curled into a smile—and let him transport her through the cottage like a sack of potatoes. Several seconds later, he swung her back down, her bare feet sinking into the parlor's plush area rug. The room she'd avoided for days now felt like the most natural place in the world.

And although the Steinway still couldn't move or speak or do anything other than sit there like the inanimate object it was, Mia could've sworn she heard a faint message of approval.

Way to go, maestro.

His deft hands unhooked her bra and then found the zipper at the back of her skirt, both garments falling to her feet. Fully nude, she pushed his boxer briefs down a sturdy set of legs, and his impressive erection jutted out from a thatch of tawny hair. She sank to her knees, satisfaction surging when his chest hitched. Keeping her eyes locked on his, she gently kissed the tip of his cock, and his hips bucked like a randy schoolboy.

Oh, he wanted this bad. And after he'd orchestrated her undoing at the DT, there was nothing she wanted more than to level the playing field. To watch him fall apart.

Two can play that game, Boss Man.

With agonizing restraint, she puckered her lips and placed soft kisses along the length of his shaft. And then she stuck out her tongue and licked the underside of his cock, coating the rigid skin with wetness. Back and forth, back and forth.

Travis groaned helplessly. "Oh God, please just suck it. Don't torture me."

"But it's so much fun," she whispered with a saucy smile. "Torturing you, that is."

Cupping his balls in her hand, she reveled in how his guttural sounds grew deeper. "Mia, please, for the love of God."

"That's what you get for slapping my ass."

"Don't act like you didn't love it."

"And for making me scream into your hand in a public restroom."

A cheeky grin accompanied his reply. "Wasn't that your idea?"

No way he was getting the last word. She took his cock as far down her throat as she could manage, clasping her lips around the hard column of flesh in a fervent suck.

"*Fuck,*" he bellowed, fists clenching.

Pulling back, she released his erection with a loud *pop.* "You were saying?" she prompted.

He shook his head hastily. "I wasn't saying anything."

"Good."

That settled, she returned to the task at hand and

bobbed her head with enthusiasm, working her hand in tandem with the movement of her mouth. His breath labored as she got messy with it, her saliva coating his cock. Unable to string a proper sentence together, he bestowed her with some of the most colorful epithets she'd ever heard. Especially once her free hand crept between her legs to rub her aching clit. The sight of her pleasuring herself while sucking him off became too much for him to bear, as he soon motioned for her to stand.

"Hold on. One second. I—fuck, Mia. That's good. I'm gonna come if you keep this up."

"That's kind of the point," she quipped, licking the sexy grooves of his hipbones.

"I'm not some young stud." He pulled her to her feet with an abashed grin. "It'll take me a while to get hard again if I blow now."

"We have all the time in the world," she reminded him, throwing her arms over his muscular shoulders. "All night and tomorrow and—"

The elephant stampeded into the room, and she stopped abruptly. Sure, they had time. Several weeks of it. But they didn't have all the time in the world. Still, they'd already wordlessly addressed this at the DT. They were both adults, and they knew exactly what this was—a nice, torrid fling. A way to take the edge off for a few weeks.

So why did the thought of leaving him make her chest feel like it was a roof collapsing under the force of a terrible tempest?

The shift in her mood didn't go unnoticed. "Still with me?" he murmured.

Her voice cracked only slightly. "Yeah. Sorry. Just thinking."

"Oh, we can't have that."

Laughing despite herself, she pinched his abdomen. "Shut up."

He faux gasped, and they pretended to tussle for a few moments. But then a thought occurred to him, and his head fell back with frustration.

"Ah, hell," he bemoaned. "Give me a second."

"Where are you going?" she asked, brows narrowing as he went to exit.

"My pants are in the kitchen. With my wallet. And the lone condom that's been in there for ages. And it better not be fucking expired. Otherwise, I'm gonna shit a brick."

Mia snorted with laughter as he charged out of the room bare-ass naked. Then she said a silent prayer that the condom was safe to use, since the last thing she'd expected when packing for this trip was a steamy dalliance, and she had no protection other than her birth control pills.

Returning in record time, with his impressive erection leading the way, he waved the foil packet in triumph. "All good."

A relieved gust of air left her lungs. But Travis wasn't ready to move to the main event yet, as he perched her on the arm of the couch. It went without saying that the man wasn't one to shy away from a healthy bit of manhandling, and she certainly had no objections when he opened her legs and folded one back, planting her foot atop the sofa.

Sinking to his haunches, he purred, "My turn."

He planted his face between her thighs, his tongue immediately lapping at her wet folds. Whimpers pealed from her as she ran her fingers through his hair, gripping the tresses for leverage as she rocked against his mouth. He licked her pussy and suckled her clit with gusto, and her arousal surged, but each time she teetered on the edge of an orgasm, he pulled back.

She couldn't take it anymore, her head jerking around with frustration. "Travis, stop fucking around and make me come."

A rakish laugh echoed from him as he stood, pulling her from the sofa and draping her body against his to hold her close. His stiff cock poked against her belly as he mercilessly squeezed her ass cheeks.

"Listen to me," he whispered into her ear. "I've wanted to fuck you since the moment I saw you on the porch, looking down on me like I didn't belong."

Shame ballooned within her. "Travis—"

"Ah, ah, ah." His scolding was accompanied by a smack on her bottom. "Let me finish."

Her head fell to his shoulder, and she nodded helplessly.

The tone of his voice was gravel and grit as he continued. "But this is *my* town. And the next time you come, it's going to be thanks to my cock. Got it?"

There was no pride left in her. No fight remained. All she wanted was him, so she said, "Yes. I understand."

The foil packet in his hand was ripped open, and he sheathed his cock with the condom. Then he strode to the piano bench and took a seat, facing away from the keys.

"Hop on," he drawled, dipping his head for emphasis.

Such a sexual directive, and one she was helpless to resist. She straddled him, the bench thankfully long enough to accommodate her knees, and he caught one nipple between his lips as she notched his cock against her entrance. Her inner muscles rioted as she sank down, his thickness invading. An onslaught of stimulation rocketed through her when she reached the hilt and rose to establish a cadence. His large hands clung to her ass, aiding her rhythm as she rode him like her life depended on it.

Her nails dug into his shoulders, and he hissed with pleasure, his eyes constantly darting from her face to her bouncing breasts. He thrust into her as she bared down on his cock, desperate to get deeper with each movement. Their earlier heated banter ceased completely, both at a loss for words as they rocked together.

Her orgasm was a ticking time bomb destined to explode, and every inch of him brought her closer and closer to climax. Desperate for release, she slid her hand between her legs. One, two, three strokes of her clit, and she exploded like a firecracker. Overpowering contractions careened through her, and she sagged against him with a broken sob of pleasure.

Once somewhat coherent, she lifted her head and her eyes fluttered open. A searing blue gaze found hers, his jaw slack with astonishment. Sweat covered his brow, his dark-blond strands of hair were mussed and wild, and his rugged beauty stole her breath.

"You good?" he asked, the question so soft she almost didn't hear it.

She nodded faintly, overcome with emotion at the sincere check-in.

He kneaded her breasts together and pinched the stiff nipples. "Can you take more?"

"You know it," she replied with a saucy grin.

Seductive laughter vibrated from him, and he kept her body close to help her stand. True to form, he positioned her to his liking, encouraging her to bend over the bench and arch her back as he situated himself behind her.

"Oh fuck," she cried out when he entered her swiftly. Not an ounce of mercy was shown, his hips pulling back and returning with another deep thrust, and she reached forward in search of something steady.

Her hands slammed onto the piano keys, a racket of indeterminate noise echoing through the room as he pounded her from behind. As his hands gripped her shoulders for leverage, she adjusted to his relentless rhythm and drove her hips back to meet his movements.

"Fuck yeah, move back onto me," he growled, one hand capturing her heap of curls. He tugged her head back to rumble in her ear, "I'm gonna nut if you keep that up."

"Yes, yes, yes. Oh *fuck.*"

Their bodies slapped together, and her whimpers increased while his feral grunts grew more extreme, culminating in a beautifully brutal symphony. Soon enough, the crescendo arrived as he climaxed with a ragged roar. His athletic frame jerked as he emptied himself into the condom, both panting like a pair of wild animals.

Once he reoriented, he withdrew from her and quickly disposed of the rubber in a nearby wastebasket. Her legs were jelly, and she slumped onto the piano bench, bringing her hand to her chest in an attempt to ease her racing heart.

A throw blanket sat atop the love seat, and Travis unfurled it with a flourish, placing it onto the floor. He sank down unceremoniously, and she followed suit, both beyond spent. She stretched out alongside him, the fuzzy blanket tickling her skin. Her heart rate had mostly returned to normal, but as he pulled her close and pressed a kiss against her temple, it stirred again.

"Holy fuck," he breathed out in a daze.

For some reason, she found his reaction hilarious. Giggles bubbled up and tumbled from her mouth.

He nudged her and asked, "What's so funny?"

"You sound stunned."

"Well, it's been a while. Sue me."

She raised her head to find his gaze. "How long?"

"Like a year or two."

"Wait a minute," she said, sitting straight up. "Are you serious? You? Mr. Seduction over here hadn't had sex in *years*?"

He flopped his arms out like a sacrifice. "Why do you think I laid it on so thick?"

Her giggles reemerged and altered into full-blown guffaws as she laid back down, easily fitting against the shape of his body. He wrapped one arm around her and squeezed.

"Besides, you were..." Trailing off, he sighed, his soft breath tickling her right cheek as he attempted to find the words. "Well, you were you."

Time passed, and the easy silence was as comfortable as the cozy blanket beneath them. Until a thought danced its way into her head.

She turned to lock eyes with him. "What were you going to ask me?"

"Huh?"

"Our wager. If you'd won the pool game. What would you have asked me?"

His stare softened, as did his voice. "I was going to ask if you'd play the piano for me."

Emotion lodged in her throat, rendering her mute for several seconds. The earnest confession touched something deep within her, and she nuzzled against his steady chest for comfort. Thankfully, he didn't push her. His fingers simply skimmed the curve of her spine as she inhaled a few fortifying breaths.

Her mouth opened, but nothing emerged, and she thought of the quote from composer Jean Sibelius.

"Music begins where the possibilities of language end."

She might not have the words, but she had her talent,

and in her heart of hearts, she knew the time was now. Full of resolve, she rose and stepped to the bench. Naked as the day she was born, she sat and placed her hands on the keys.

Her lack of clothes was nothing compared to how her soul was stripped bare as she began to play one of her early compositions. Something separate from her ex-husband. Something she hadn't played in years. Nevertheless, she revisited the stirring sonata while nude, in a small coastal town she had no true connection to, and in the company of a complicated man who was destined to disappear from her life. And, somehow, it was exactly what she needed.

When she played the final note, there was no thunderous applause. No rapturous calls for an encore. But she felt more content and accomplished than she'd felt in years. Because she had never needed the applause. Never wanted the fame and adulation. All that had ever mattered was the music and how it made her feel blessedly alive.

A gentle kiss graced the small of her back, the touch featherlight. Her throat tightened at the gentle gesture, and she blinked rapidly to dispel the stinging tears threatening to escape.

"That was..." Travis paused, unable to find the words. "Wow."

Swallowing down a whirlwind of emotion, she took a moment so her voice wouldn't shake. "Thank you."

"Can you teach me?"

The quiet question was a surprise, and when she glanced over her shoulder to find him kneeling on the ground like a willing supplicant, her heart almost burst from her chest and into his calloused hands.

"I'd like that," she said with a tiny nod.

She scooted to one side of the bench to provide enough room for him to sit beside her. Both of them naked in more ways than one, she coached him through a simple tune: "Twinkle Twinkle Little Star."

Their hands glided together over the keys, her movements assured and confident, his clumsy and unsure. But she was patient, and he listened, and soon, he got the hang of it. When he finished the chords of the nursery rhyme without her assistance, he looked at her with a proud smile.

"Not bad for a roofer, huh?" he joked.

She rested her chin against his shoulder and said, "Not bad at all."

And as the stars shimmered outside and the waves lapped against the rocks, music adorned the cottage into the late hours of the night.

SIX

The following days were a haze of lust and laughter.

It was almost alarming how easily they settled into a pseudo-domestic life together. How Travis kissed her goodbye each morning before heading to the office to manage operations. The way her phone pinged with silly and sweet text messages throughout the day. Evenings spent preparing dinner together, Mia no longer solely delegated to the role of chef. Endless cuddles on the couch as they talked about everything and nothing. And nights filled with soul-searing desire, their bodies joining together as if made for each other.

But the heady rush of a new relationship wasn't the sole reason she was on cloud nine—her musical mojo had returned with a bang.

Pun intended.

Inspiration teemed from her, and Mia spent hours at the piano every day, working on her first new piece of music in months. Although still a work in progress, the arrangement encapsulated the emotions she'd experienced since arriving in town—everything from defeat to exuberance to passion.

She titled it "Daymont Days."

At the end of her second week at the cottage, she sucked it up and had a long conference call with Leslie. They mapped out her next steps, both agreeing that it was better to pursue other avenues instead of jumping right back into the jungle that was New York's musical theatre scene. Leslie's brother-in-law was dating an independent filmmaker who needed a composer to score her next film, and she floated the idea of an introductory meeting, which Mia was all for.

After ending the call, Mia closed her laptop with a cautiously optimistic smile. After months of missing the mark, things were finally starting to look up.

Or so she thought. A sharp ache manifested in her stomach, the cramps signaling the arrival of Aunt Flow. Her birth control pills helped ease the pain of her period, but the first day remained unpleasant when all was said and done. Mood plummeting, she headed upstairs to her bedroom to change out of her jeans. *Sweatpants or bust.*

An unsettling reality tugged at her heart as she stripped her legs out of the denim. Sex would have to cease for at least a night. She was no stranger to fucking while riding the red wave, but cramps and bloating did not make a girl feel desirable.

And then a depressing thought jumped into her head.

Maybe Travis won't even want to see me at all.

Perhaps not the most rational conclusion, but they'd had sex each night since that explosive first encounter, unable to keep their hands off each other. Physical attraction had been the initial catalyst, and she worried that its absence would translate to faded interest on his part. Insecurity grabbed her lungs and didn't let go as she soberly slipped her legs into a pair of fleece Juilliard sweatpants.

As she crouched down and rummaged through her luggage to assess her tampon inventory, her phone buzzed with a text message from Travis.

Stopping by a project site for a bit, then heading to you.

She plopped onto the carpeted ground, crossing her legs and leaning back against the side of the bed. Her already roiling gut tightened further as she typed out a reply.

Okay. Just FYI, my monthly visitor came, so won't be up for any bed sport tonight. Sorry.

Foolish tears arose as she waited for an answer that didn't come, but she pushed them down and grabbed her granny's sweater, swathing herself in the threadbare cardigan. Then she padded down to the den and burrowed beneath the cozy blanket, her body melting into the couch. Across the room, the television blared with a mindless disaster movie as the sun started to set. Streaks of vibrant oranges and rich pinks swirled in the sky, but her mood remained pitch-black.

Sometime later, keys hit the kitchen counter, the sharp sound traveling down the hallway, and her head perked up. Travis appeared within seconds, his lean form moving through the shadows of the room.

"Hey," he murmured, lifting her legs to take a seat on the couch. He draped them over his lap and squeezed her thighs gently. "How you feeling?"

A bit befuddled, she asked, "What are you doing here?"

His brow furrowed, the flashing lights from the television flittering over his features. "What do you mean, what am I doing here?"

Throat clogged with emotion, she collected herself. Her hands covered her eyes, kneading back maudlin tears as she shook her head. "Sorry. Period brain. I'm glad you're here."

He puffed his chest out like a peacock. "Damn right, you are."

Giggling, she nudged his thigh with her foot, and then a comfortable silence fell over them as they watched the last few minutes of the film.

As the credits rolled, he turned to her. "Figured we could order a pizza for dinner. Sound good?"

She agreed with a nod. "I could definitely go for some carbs right now."

Cheesy and greasy glory arrived a half hour later, and even Mia—the ultimate New Yorker—had to admit that Connecticut could make a mean pizza pie. Not only was her belly full, but her heart was as well because, after dinner, Travis took it upon himself to search every closet and storage space for a heating pad. The triumphant shout that echoed through the cottage once he located one made her cramps feel suspiciously like butterflies.

When they retired to bed later that night, her eyes landed on the nightstand. She'd left her phone there all evening, and the home screen burned bright with a message from Leslie, delivered hours earlier.

> Just spoke to my BIL. His GF would love to do an in-person meeting. Remind me when you're back in the city again?

The innocuous question made Mia's blood run cold, and in the recesses of her mind, a faint sound formed.

Ticktock. Ticktock.

"You okay, baby?" Travis asked, brushing his fingers across her back.

She gulped and placed the phone back down. "All good."

Snuggled with him beneath the covers, she lay awake for hours. His steady, sleep-filled breaths filled the air, but those soothing sounds were no match for the ticking clock hovering over their relationship.

HER PERIOD CAME AND WENT, but sadly, so did the days. In fact, they grew shorter as the season inched further into October, the sun setting earlier and earlier. Nevertheless, their idyllic yet doomed domesticity remained strong, and Mia's ability to compartmentalize also strengthened. Her afternoons were still spent creating music and making business plans with Leslie, but Maestro Mia disappeared the moment Travis walked through the door each evening with his easygoing gait and roguish grin.

By the time her final week at the cottage rolled around, she'd refused to acknowledge that the relationship was living on borrowed time, and she knew it would hurt all the more as a result.

On the Sunday morning before her scheduled departure, he spent a full thirty minutes eating her out, edging her to the point of madness. Body contorted with passion and the sheets damp with her sweat, she seized, and a hoarse cry ripped from her throat as her orgasm detonated.

The man was the ultimate distraction. No wonder she'd been able to ignore the inevitable.

He crawled up the length of her body. "Would it be weird if I said I'm still hungry?"

Laughter burst from her. "No. I'm starving too. What do you want to do for breakfast?"

His head turned to consult the digital clock on the nightstand. "The bakery's open. It gets busy on Sundays, but it's still early. You game for coffee and pastries?"

"Only always," she quipped, kissing him on the tip of his nose.

After a quick rinse in the shower, she returned to the bedroom, stopping short at his solemn posture.

"Your phone was buzzing," he murmured, gesturing over to the nightstand where it sat with the screen facing up.

Missed Call from Leslie.

A knot formed in her throat, but she swallowed it down and quickly threw a sweater dress over her head. "I'll call her back later," she insisted, plastering a reassuring smile on her face.

He met her smile with a cautious one of his own, both unwilling to discuss the inescapable truth, and they headed outside to hop in his truck. While on the journey downtown, her phone vibrated again, the soft sound somehow as jarring as a jackhammer.

"You can answer it," he told her in a hush.

Mia shook her head vehemently as she rummaged in her purse. "I'll just text her."

Hands shaking, she sent off a terse message that she couldn't chat, and Leslie responded immediately with news about the meeting scheduled for the following week. Apparently, their travel plans had changed.

Can you make this Friday work?

That would mean returning to the city a full day earlier than expected. A minor ask, yet it made tears spring to her eyes, but she sucked it up and replied back in the affirmative.

Yes, I'll make it work.

"All good?" he asked once she placed her phone back in her purse.

"All good," she lied in a whisper.

The truck pulled into a parking spot about a block away from the bakery, and leaves crunched beneath their shoes as they walked over. Throwing his arm over her shoulder, he pulled her closer, and giddiness pulsed through her veins. The rush was so intoxicating that Leslie's request fluttered from her mind, and she didn't even flinch as they passed the Daymont Symphony School.

When Travis reached for the door's handle, it whooshed open, and a man stepped out. And although Mia had never laid eyes on him before, his identity was plain as day.

Thomas. Travis's brother.

The resemblance was uncanny. The Flynn brothers shared the same height and body type, with lean muscles born from physical labor. Their bone structure was near identical—the same proud nose and chiseled jawline—and their hair color matched to a T. But the similarities ended there. No doubt, the elder brother was more clean-cut, his shaven face a stark contrast to Travis's tawny stubble. Dressed impeccably for a Sunday morning, Thomas wore tan chinos and a navy cable-knit sweater to ward off the October chill, whereas Travis donned ratty jeans and his tried-and-true hoodie. Polar opposites in every way.

The brothers sized each other up for several seconds, like two outlaws before an old-timey shootout, with Mia a reluctant bystander. God willing, she wouldn't get caught in the crossfire.

"Trav," Thomas said with a nod.

Travis cut his brother a stone-cold stare before replying with a clipped "Tommy."

Thomas's eyes—the exact same shade of blue—flickered over to Mia, no doubt noting their chummy pose. While his perusal wasn't overtly judgmental, there was a sternness to his energy, and the eldest-sibling vibes were downright strong. But then Mia cracked through the austere bearing and realized what he was waiting for—an introduction.

Her stomach took a nosedive when Travis remained silent, the episode shifting from uncomfortable to unbearable. After a few excruciating seconds, Thomas got the hint and spared a tight smile before leaving.

Despite his brother's departure, the atmosphere didn't relax, tension radiating from Travis's shoulders. She glanced at him warily as he opened the door for her, curious if he'd acknowledge the encounter, but he remained tight-lipped as they stepped inside, and the smell of sugary goodness didn't ease the sting of his lack of introduction.

Awkwardness persisted as they placed their order at the counter. Both opted for savory instead of sweet, ordering ham-and-cheese croissants alongside massive coffees. Moments later, the cashier returned with their items, and Mia didn't put up a fight when Travis pulled out his wallet to pay.

They situated themselves at a circular patio table out on the sidewalk, as every spot inside the bakery was occupied. The blustery autumn wind was fitting for the fraught interlude, and she zipped up her leather jacket. He sat with a weary sigh and stretched out his legs before taking a hearty bite of his croissant.

A few more minutes passed, and then she couldn't take it anymore. "I guess that was your brother, huh?"

"Good guess."

His voice was flat, his frequent teasing lilt now dead and gone. She removed the lid from her coffee to let it cool, blowing at the liquid before taking a tentative sip.

"You didn't introduce me," she muttered.

His eyes shot up like a cannon to find her gaze, confusion written in his expression. "Why would I introduce you?"

The question was sincere, and perhaps that was why it felt like a knife to her heart. Because he had a point. Why would he introduce his brother to a woman he'd been fucking for a few weeks when she was leaving town in mere days?

Ticktock. Ticktock.

"Never mind," she mumbled, pulling apart the gooey croissant with her hands.

"I told you I wasn't close to my family."

"Says the man who has their coat of arms tattooed on his skin."

His jaw sagged into a stunned expression. Then his stare hardened, and he leaned back, crossing his arms over his chest. "When do you head back to the city again?"

What was another knife to the heart when all was said and done? Still, she shoved down the pain and shrugged. "Few days."

And, just like that, the conversation was over. They ate breakfast without another word, sipping at their coffees until nothing remained in the paper cups. Even with the friction, he remained the unlikely gentleman she knew him to be, disposing of her trash and then opening the passenger door for her once it was time to return home.

Home.

The realization knocked the wind out of her. Over the past few weeks, the coastal cottage had morphed from a simple hideaway—a place where she could get her head back on straight—into a genuine home where unlikely magic had happened. And perhaps the most stunning was how the man beside her had wormed his way into her heart, and how helpless she'd been to stop it.

But when the truck lumbered up the driveway and Travis didn't unbuckle his seat belt, she knew it was over.

"Thanks for breakfast," she choked out.

"Sure."

Her hand hovered over the handle, unable to open the door. How could she, when everything felt so unfinished? When so many things were left unsaid? But most crushing was how she hadn't performed her latest composition for him. She'd been holding it close, waiting until each note was perfect before presenting it to the man who'd been her inspiration.

Never in her wildest dreams would she have imagined that a devilishly brash roofer would become a maestro's muse. How the smiles he bestowed had rebuilt her confidence. How each touch of his rugged hands helped bring her back to life. She should've known better than to write this off as two adults indulging in a simple fling. Nothing was ever going to be simple, not when it came to this man.

"Mia..." He trailed off, keeping his eyes on the water in the distance. His chest rose and fell with a heavy breath before he said, "Just go. Okay?"

It was a plea. A prayer not to prolong this. To put them both out of their misery. And maybe it was better that way. No emotional discussion, no teary goodbyes. Just two people who knew the score finally reaching the end of the road.

As much as it physically pained her, she opened the door and descended from the truck. Each step toward the house felt like bare feet on broken glass, but she didn't cry until the door was closed behind her.

SEVEN

On her final evening in Daymont, Mia drove downtown to purchase a premade salad from the market. No food remained in the refrigerator, and after the joy the cottage's kitchen had brought her, wilted lettuce for dinner was a dismal disappointment.

Woe had taken up residence the last few days, the home devoid of any laughter or joy. She continued tinkering with her new composition, but each note now felt trite and tiresome, and the irony wasn't lost on her. How fitting to end her stay in Daymont the same uninspiring way it had started.

Nevertheless, she secretly hoped for...something. A sign, perhaps. A bit naive, but she couldn't help but wish for some nebulous force to push her toward the right path. Because, even after her strangely subdued separation from Travis, the thought of returning to New York left much to be desired.

After all, this town had enriched her life in a way fame and fortune never had. She didn't miss the bright lights of Broadway, the red-carpet functions, or the industry gossip.

The weeks away from the world of Maestro Mia had allowed regular old Mia Pelletier to have her time in the spotlight, and she was loath to throw in the towel now.

But the absence of Travis lingered, and she remembered his words from their first night together. This was his town. She was always meant to be nothing more than a visitor.

While returning to her car with salad in hand, her focus landed on the Daymont Symphony School, and regret festered like an untreated wound. But, as if by fate, the school's door opened, and she smiled at a familiar face.

Eric, the foreman from Travis's crew, ushered a preteen girl through the door and out onto the sidewalk. The spitting image of him, with identical vivid red hair and freckles, Eric's daughter slung her backpack onto one shoulder and pushed circular wire-rim glasses further up the bridge of her nose. Noticing Mia, she stopped dead in her tracks, her jaw dropping to reveal a mouth of braces.

"Mia, hey!" Eric greeted before sending his daughter a knowing smile. "I didn't realize you were still in town."

"Leaving tomorrow," she said, both words full of quiet misery.

"Dad, oh my God," Eric's daughter squeaked. "You said you knew somebody who knew somebody who knew somebody. That's how you got my playbill signed. That's what you said!"

"Yeah, well." Eric shrugged and then admitted, "I lied."

Mia laughed at the simple explanation and then said, "Don't blame your dad. I asked him to keep it hush-hush." She held out her hand for a proper introduction. "I'm Mia."

In a daze, Eric's daughter shook her hand limply. "Oh my God. Wow. Hi. I'm Alice."

The hairs on the back of Mia's neck stood up, and she struggled to pull in a breath.

If you were looking for a sign that this is where you're supposed to be...I think you just found one.

"That was my granny's name," Mia choked out in a whisper. She took a second to compose herself, hand falling to her side before a smile returned in full force. "It's nice to meet you, Alice."

"You too. Sorry, I know it's annoying, but can I get a picture?"

Mia nodded, and they posed in front of the music school. Dutiful dad Eric took several pictures from different angles, and Alice inspected the images before declaring his photography adequate. Then Alice launched into an overview of her lessons—she'd tried the piano, the violin, and the flute before focusing her efforts on the piano, much to Mia's delight.

"It's a good school," Eric told Mia, gesturing to the colorful decals decorating the windows. "Hopefully, you can come back and visit again one day. Maybe experience it firsthand."

"I have a feeling you haven't seen the last of me," she replied, buzzing with bliss.

On the drive back to the cottage, she relayed a silent thanks to her grandmother. She had never considered herself a spiritual or religious person, but there was no denying that her granny remained with her even in death, and nowhere had that connection felt stronger than during the past weeks in Daymont.

It was the final sign Mia needed to take the leap—a leap toward a life of music on her own modest and magnificent terms. And, if all went well, a life with the charismatic man who'd challenged her, inspired her, and helped rediscover that passion.

Flipping the blinker on, she turned the last corner

toward the cottage. If Travis didn't answer the phone, she'd track him down in person, starting with the DT. But that plan became moot when she pulled into the driveway, her heart skipping a beat at the sight of his green truck.

He sat on the porch steps, with his head hanging and his elbows resting on his knees. A rhapsody of epic proportions burst from her chest as she stepped out of the car, their gazes meeting as he raised his head. Immediately shooting to his feet, he shifted his stance back and forth in a nervous manner as she approached.

"Hey," he mumbled. "I, uh...I realized that I didn't return the spare key."

A lone key sat in the center of his outstretched palm. She'd given him the spare after their first night together so he could come and go as he pleased, trusting him implicitly. Trusting *them*.

Instead of taking the key, Mia ascended the stairs and plastered herself against his body, draping her arms over his shoulders for a hug. After being underwater for days, the sensation of his strong biceps circling her was like breaching the surface. His hands shifted to tilt her head back, planting a panty-dropping kiss on her mouth, and not a smidgen of doubt remained in her heart.

"This is fucking selfish of me to say," he grunted against her lips, "but goddamn it, I don't want you to go."

"I'm not going anywhere," she assured him breathlessly.

He took an incredulous step back. "But you—"

"Yeah, I technically have the house until tomorrow, but it's not like anyone's moving in right after me," she explained, knowing her agent only rented to the public during the busy summer season. "I'm sure I can work something out with Leslie for the time being."

"Mia, come on. You can't prolong this forever. You have a career to think about."

She cocked an eyebrow at him. "Didn't you just say you don't want me to go?"

"Trust me, I don't. The thought fucking kills me." A weary breath left his mouth, and he held up the tiny key to the cottage between his thumb and index finger. "Hell, I nearly jumped out of my skin when I realized I had a convenient excuse to come see you."

With a tender smile, she took the key and placed it back into the center of his palm, folding his fingers over it to keep it safe.

The column of his throat bobbed. "I want you here, but I also don't want you giving things up for me. You're—" He stopped to steady his emotions, inhaling deeply. Wonder shone in his eyes as he finished his thought. "You're kind of a big fucking deal."

Her hands traced the line of his jaw, savoring the prickling sensation of the bristles. She cupped his face and whispered, "I just want to be a big fucking deal to you."

His head sagged with a relieved sigh, their foreheads touching gently. They breathed in tandem, the sound of the river in the distance a perfect soundtrack for the tender moment. But uncertainty and guilt still radiated from him, so Mia ushered him down onto the porch steps. Sitting side by side, she pleaded her case.

"I can compose music anywhere. I don't have to be in New York to do that. It helps, sure, but it's not the be-all and end-all. The piano in there has served me fine the last few weeks," she said, nodding toward the house with a smile. "Besides, I've always wanted to teach. Like my granny."

"I can attest you'd be great at that," he confirmed.

His face shone with memories of their first night

together. How she'd coached him through the nursery rhyme, both of them so strong in their naked vulnerability. The remembrance warmed her and buoyed her toward her main point.

"When I first came here, I felt like I needed to prove myself, you know? Compose some brilliant piece of music so I could return to the city triumphant. Put Maestro Mia back on the pedestal. But for what?" She shook her head, wondering how she'd ever been so consumed by her pride and ego. "That wouldn't have made me happy. I don't have to be Maestro Mia with you. I can just be Mia. *And* I can still have music."

Travis took in her words, his tight features softening. "Well, I know better than to argue with you," he joked.

That pulled a laugh out of her, and she nudged him with her elbow. He searched her face, his mouth opening and closing several times as words failed him.

"I kind of acted like a dick the last time I saw you," he blurted out.

She scrunched up her face in faux confusion. "Kind of?"

Now it was his turn to give her a teasing nudge, but she took the opportunity to pull him closer, knowing support was needed for his mea culpa.

"It's not that I didn't want to introduce you to my brother. But what the hell was I supposed to say? Hey, Tommy, this is the woman I'm absolutely wild for, and she'll be leaving my ass soon." He stopped and cracked his knuckles, sorrow pulsating from each word. "Like before."

"You don't have to worry about that, because I've already told you that I'm not going anywhere," she whispered fiercely in his ear. Then she rubbed her hand up and down his back. "But I hope things get better with your brother. Maybe one day."

He scoffed, although Mia knew hope was still within him, buried deep down inside. "I guess we'll see."

Better than flat-out denial. Beggars couldn't be choosers, so she'd take it. She knew firsthand that special things could happen in this town, so she tucked away her faith for a Flynn brothers' reconciliation. Stranger things had happened.

As the sun disappeared, Travis found her gaze again and stared at her with amazement. "So we're really gonna do this?" he asked. "You and me?"

"Sure are, Boss Man."

With a growl, he pulled her into his lap and brought his mouth to hers for a scorching kiss. Mia didn't know what the next few days, weeks, or months would bring, but uncertainty disappeared thanks to his talented lips. Stirred into a frenzy, she rocked her pelvis against his rapidly hardening erection, mewling with need.

"Let's get inside before the neighbors call the cops," Travis said with a laugh, pulling her to her feet.

They stumbled to the back door, his spare key coming in handy. Once inside the kitchen, he slammed the door and pressed her against it, crowding her willing body.

"First, fucking. Then dinner," he stated. *God love a man with a plan.* Buttons slipped through their loops despite his fumbling fingers, until her shirt was finally splayed open. "What should we make?"

She burst into giggles. "There's a sad salad sitting in the car. I don't have any food in the house."

That beloved cheeky grin of his returned as he tossed her blouse to the side. "How about the DT?"

SUMMER HAD ARRIVED IN DAYMONT, along with the tourists. The seasonal hotspots lining the coast opened as visitors invaded post-Memorial Day weekend, and after a life-changing autumn, a cozy winter, and a scenic spring, Mia got to experience her new home in all its summertime glory.

But even with the flashy new restaurants to enjoy, Mia would always prefer the DT.

Dee slammed an IPA onto the sticky bar as Mia thanked her with a demure smile, the memories of her bathroom hookup with Travis ever present. After a large gulp of beer, she sat back in her stool and sighed heavily. It had been a long week, and it wasn't over yet. Daymont Symphony School's annual piano recital was the following evening, and anxiety had ruled the roost during that afternoon's final dress rehearsal. Mia adored her students beyond measure, so much so that she'd internalized their angst and stage fright.

Nevertheless, each day spent in the school's studios was proof that she'd made the right choice to stay in Daymont. For the first time in ages, her notoriety had worked to her advantage when she walked into the school to ask if they were hiring, soon after reconciling with Travis. After the initial shock, the owner had recovered quickly and asked if she could start that weekend.

Leslie hadn't been thrilled at Mia's change of plans, but she'd allowed her to stay at the cottage under one condition: that Mia honor her commitment to meet with the independent film director. Instead of returning to New York, they'd met via video call and surprisingly hit it off. But after the discussion, Mia knew she wasn't the right choice for that specific film, although she promised to stay in touch in the hopes they could collaborate in the future.

When the weather started to turn, she moved out of Leslie's waterside cottage so renters could take advantage and her agent could turn a profit on the house. She missed it terribly sometimes, but Travis's two-bedroom, single-story ranch home suited her just as well.

Speak of the devil. He slid onto the stool beside her and leaned in to brush his mouth against hers. "Hey, baby."

"Hey, yourself. Funny seeing you here."

He grinned and ordered his own beer. While waiting for their plate of nachos, they chatted about minor topics, but his right leg continually bounced like a jackhammer. By now, she'd learned all his quirks, and the nonstop tremors hinted that he yearned to make a confession.

The plate of cheesy chips arrived, and she bit the bullet. "You look like you want to say something," she coaxed, scooping a handful of nachos onto her plate.

Travis found her gaze in the mirror. "I love you, you know."

Her heart fluttered like a hummingbird as she kept her eyes on his reflection. "I know. I love you too."

"I invited Thomas to the recital."

Her neck cracked as she whipped her head toward him, her shock impossible to disguise. "You did?"

"I hope that's okay."

Hastily, she wiped her messy hands with her napkin and grabbed hold of his sturdy forearm, squeezing in a supportive manner. "Of course it's okay."

While she'd met Travis's parents and brother over the holidays, it had been a particularly tense Christmas Eve dinner, and things remained precarious. But Mia didn't want to push, so she let him set the tone with his family while secretly hoping he'd take baby steps toward a better relationship.

This wasn't simply a baby step. It was a huge step, and her fragile hope for reconciliation strengthened.

Travis stuffed some chips into his mouth and chewed. "And he invited us to dinner after. At the Club House."

Her brows jumped up into her hairline. "The one at the yacht club?"

"One and the same. Do you wanna go?"

"Sure. Yeah." Mia paused and then shot him a look. "Do *you* want to go?"

The moment seemed to stretch out forever as she waited for his response. Until, finally, Travis shrugged his broad shoulders and replied, "Could be fun."

Awash with joy, she leaned in to kiss his cheek and whispered, "I think it's gonna be a good summer."

ACKNOWLEDGMENTS

Behind every great author is a brilliant editor, and I'm fortunate to work with the best. Brooklyn, thank you for everything. I've learned so much from you, and there's no doubt I would've given up if you hadn't talked me off the ledge all those months ago. Thank you for always having my back and for fixing my comma placements.

I'm so grateful to every early reader who provided feedback and helped me shape these novellas into something I'm proud of. Special thanks to Rachel Rowan for being my confidant during all three stories, and to Becky and Andrea for helping with Mallory and Joel.

Cassie—many thanks for your design expertise. It never fails to amaze me how you take my vague descriptions and create the perfect cover.

Much love to my family and friends, and—as always—a special thank-you to my parents for never wavering in their support of this little dream of mine.

ABOUT THE AUTHOR

Brianna Bancroft is a trained playwright turned romance novelist. Born and raised in New Jersey, she enjoys vintage clothing, ballet, and bourbon. Visit her website to subscribe to her newsletter and receive regular updates.

Made in the USA
Columbia, SC
11 June 2025

59303577R00155